THEIR RELUCTANT BRIDE

BRIDGEWATER MÉNAGE SERIES - BOOK 6

VANESSA VALE

Copyright © 2016 by Vanessa Vale

This is a work of fiction. Names, characters, places and incidents are the products of the author's imagination and used fictitiously. Any resemblance to actual persons, living or dead, businesses, companies, events or locales is entirely coincidental.

All rights reserved.

No part of this book may be reproduced in any form or by any electronic or mechanical means, including information storage and retrieval systems, without written permission from the author, except for the use of brief quotations in a book review.

Cover design: Bridger Media

Cover photos: Bigstock- John Bilous; Period Images

GET A FREE BOOK!

JOIN MY MAILING LIST TO BE THE FIRST TO KNOW OF NEW RELEASES, FREE BOOKS, SPECIAL PRICES AND OTHER AUTHOR GIVEAWAYS.

http://freeromanceread.com

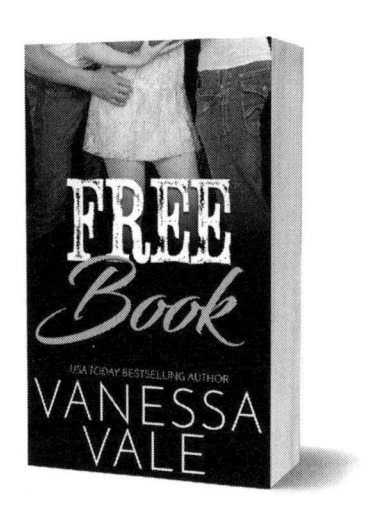

1

$\mathcal{E}$MILY

I was so nervous I could barely catch my breath. My heart pounded so frantically I was afraid it would jump right out of my chest. My fingers tingled and sweat dotted my brow. Trying to take a deep breath, I lifted my hand and wrapped on the door.

Would they even be within? It was mealtime, so perhaps they were eating with the others. I *should* be hungry, but I hadn't been able to eat a bite all day. It had taken me that long to build up enough nerve to come. I'd almost turned the horse around several times. I glanced behind me as I waited; the vast expanse of the Bridgewater Ranch was a stunning view. In the distance,

I could see another house and knew that the stables, barn and other structures were over the rise. Like all the houses on the property, they were set well apart for privacy. There was no shortage of open land on the Bridgewater Ranch.

I heard footsteps and I spun back around as the door opened. I clenched my fingers.

"Mrs. Woodhouse." Mr. Tyler wiped his hands on a dishtowel and the way his pale brow winged up, it was clear that my appearance was not expected. "You are out early. We were just finishing our lunch. Won't you please come—"

"I agree," I blurted. I couldn't hold back any longer, afraid if I did, I'd either change my mind or lose my nerve. It was petrifying, their offer of marriage, but I didn't have much of a choice and Mr. Tyler and Mr. Xander would do. Taking in how handsome the man before me was, his fair hair tousled, his blue eyes aimed solely on me, his full lips quirking up into a half smile, he would do quite nicely. If only I weren't so scared about the proposition.

"You agree?"

I closed my eyes for a moment, took a deep breath. I'd done it, I'd started the conversation, so the tightness in my chest eased, a bit. It didn't mean he wouldn't reject me, or that Mr. Xander would agree. A full day had passed. Perhaps in that time they'd changed their minds. What would I do then? "To your offer. To being fucked by both of you. I agree."

He looked at me so intently I had to glance away. It was the first time I'd ever said the word *fuck* and it felt strange. It was the word they'd used the day before. Not intercourse, not sexual congress. Fucking. I could feel my cheeks heat and I wondered if I'd ever be comfortable with saying it.

"I believe Xander would like to hear this. Won't you come in?"

I nodded and as he stepped back, I passed him into the entryway. His clean scent filled the air and I breathed it in. He didn't smell like drink as Frank had.

"Xander!" he called.

There was footfall overhead, then down the stairs. The house was very large, especially when these two men took up the space, but it wasn't theirs. It was Kane and Ian's home, along with their wife Emma. They'd gone to Billings for several days, leaving their little girl with Andrew, Robert and Ann. Mr. Tyler and Mr. Xander were staying in the vacant home during their visit to Mr. Tyler's cousin, Olivia. I was thankful that they weren't guests in her house, for I would not have the privacy I did now. This conversation was hard enough without witnesses.

I looked up and watched as Mr. Xander's long, lean body appeared one step at a time. I was able to take in the narrow waist, the long fingers, the muscular chest even before I saw his face. It was hard to look away from his chiseled jaw, the dark beard and strong brow. The few times I'd seen the man, he'd been watching me so intently it had been difficult not to squirm.

"Mrs. Woodhouse," he murmured, coming to stand before me, a little too close.

I refused to take a step back, to let the man know I was a little fearful around him. It wasn't because I was truly *afraid* of the man; he wouldn't hurt me. I worried about his effect on me. The squirming I'd done was partially because of attraction on my part. I was not used to that and it was... scary.

"Mrs. Woodhouse has said yes," Mr. Tyler told him.

Instead of his brows going up in surprise, Mr. Xander's eyes narrowed, as if he'd found his prey caught in his trap and there was nowhere to go.

"Really? Is this true, Mrs. Woodhouse?" His voice was deep, dark and promised equally dark things. This wasn't a gentle man; he was barely tamed.

I tilted my head back to look at him, for he was almost a head taller than me. I licked my lips and cleared my throat, and the words stuck there. "I agree to marry you."

"Both of us?"

I'd known what being a Bridgewater bride entailed for about half a year when Olivia had first told me. At first, I'd been stunned, for at that time I'd had no interest in the one husband I did have, and saw no need for two. But now...

"*Both* of you."

He stepped closer, and I retreated. Again. My back bumped against the closed door and he leaned in, his forearm resting beside my head. His warm breath fanned my neck. He smelled of peppermint and wood smoke. His body didn't touch me in any way and I knew if I took a deep breath, the tips of my breasts would brush against his chest.

"You understand what that will entail?" he murmured. "Whatever your husband did or didn't do with you is buried with him. We have our own expectations of a wife and we shared those with you yesterday."

I glanced at Mr. Tyler, yet felt surrounded by Mr. Xander. They were too big, too tall, too... male. I remembered all too well what those expectations were. When they'd escorted me to my ranch the day before offering marriage, I hadn't turned them down, nor had I accepted. They knew the dire straits I was in—at least some of it—and had been honorable to offer for me.

What they didn't know was that Frank's gambling debts went beyond what he owed the bank. He also owed a man named Ralph and he'd come calling, too. He wasn't honorable at all. In fact, the amount of money Frank owed him was enough to have me working on my back for months to pay it back. Ralph didn't believe a debt was repaid with my husband's death.

"What did you tell me just now?" Mr. Tyler asked, tearing me from my thoughts of Ralph.

I licked my lips again and tried to calm my racing heart, but Mr. Xander was very distracting.

"I will marry you... and, and... and fuck you both."

Mr. Xander took my hat from my head. I vaguely heard it thump on the floor, but he stroked his knuckles over my cheek. His dark eyes pierced mine and I couldn't look away. "You're not a virgin," he said. It wasn't a question.

I shook my head. I hadn't been one for quite some time. I wasn't a naive virgin for them to deflower.

"Then we don't have to worry about you being a reluctant bride, do we?"

I wasn't so sure about that. I was *very* reluctant, but I also had never been as eager for a man's touch before as I was right now. I wanted more than just the tips of his knuckles on my cheek. But two men? *These* men? I shook my head again.

"We told you that we'd fuck you. What Tyler didn't say was how he'd fill your pussy with his cock and pound into you until you came all over it. I didn't tell you that I'd breach that sweet ass of yours, shooting my seed deep inside so that you'd be dripping all day from both holes."

I gasped at the crude language and my inner muscles clenched at the picture he painted. I'd had no idea a man would put his... his cock in a bottom. I'd assumed fucking meant fumbling beneath the covers in the dark, my nightgown bunched up around my waist, just as Frank had done. Mr. Tyler would visit my bedroom one night, Mr. Xander the next. Not *that*. My cheeks heated and my nipples tightened against my corset.

"What we didn't tell you was what we'd do to you besides fucking," Mr. Tyler said. I opened my eyes—when had they fallen shut?—and saw that his gaze had darkened, his jaw was clenched tight.

"Other things besides fucking?" I wondered. What else could there be? Kissing? Frank had only rolled on top of me early in our marriage. I'd opened my legs for him and he'd push inside me, rutting, then filling me with his seed. It had been over in a minute or two. Then he began to drink and I'd been quite adept at avoiding him.

"Damn straight," Mr. Xander said. He looked at me for one short moment, then lowered himself to his knees and began lifting up the long hem of my dress.

I tried to swat his hands away, but he was not to be deterred.

"What are you doing?" I squeaked. It was one thing to agree to marry and... fuck them, but it was another to do it *right now*.

"I'm going to show you how it's going to be between us."

"Yes, but why are you on your knees? Shouldn't we be in bed? It's not dark out," I stammered, my palms pressing against the wood of the door.

He looked up at me and grinned. His teeth were white compared to his tanned skin and dark beard.

"You are a little reluctant after all."

All of a sudden, I was *very* reluctant.

"Don't worry, baby, he's going to make you feel good," Mr. Tyler said, his voice a smooth timbre. He moved closer. Backed against the door, one man at my feet and the other just beside me, I had nowhere to go.

Mr. Xander's big hands slid up my calves and knees, then my thighs, pushing the dress up as he went. More and more of me was exposed by each passing second and I shivered at the idea. Mr. Tyler took hold of the bunched-up fabric and held it up at my waist, making my lower half completely visible.

"When we marry, you won't be wearing these or needing them ever again." Mr. Xander tugged at the string on my drawers and they slid over my hips and down my legs to pool around my ankles. "Step out."

"Why?" I breathed.

"Why?" he repeated. "We will want easy access to your pussy, sweetheart."

2

EMILY

He picked up the discarded drawers and put them up on one shoulder, the thin white fabric a stark contrast to his work shirt. A dark, rusty sound escaped his throat as he looked at me... there. I darted a glance at Mr. Tyler, who was also eyeing my body. Cool air brushed against my thighs above the edge of my stockings and my woman's core was heated from their gazes. Covering myself was a waste of time. I knew with Frank that once a man had focus on intercourse, there was no dissuading. I wasn't a virgin. I knew what they wanted, what he would do. But, here? I just had to close my eyes, grit my teeth and bear it. I just had to figure out how he was doing to do it on his knees.

"I can smell her arousal from here," Mr. Xander said.

Smell me?

"Her curls, they're glistening. She's wet and we haven't even touched her yet."

"I'm not wet," I countered, embarrassed, trying to cover myself. "Mr. Xander, truly, I bathed just this morning and I don't smell, nor is my skin still damp."

"I'm just Xander." His hands cupped my ass and pulled me toward him. "If you want to be formal about it, you can call me sir, especially when I'm about to lick and finger fuck your sweet pussy. Either will do nicely."

Lick? I didn't have time to ponder his words, for his tongue flicked out and over my folds, sliding along them until he circled and circled the little bundle of nerves.

"Oh, dear Lord," I gasped, my hips bucking. I had no idea a man could—*would*—do something like this.

"Say his name, baby," Mr. Tyler whispered, kissing along the side of my neck, nipping at it and then licking the tender spot. "A man likes to hear his name when he's eating his woman's pussy."

Xander's hand dipped between my thighs to play over my... pussy as he continued to lick and suck at my tender flesh. I gripped his head, tangling my fingers in his hair. I wasn't sure if it was to push him away or pull him closer.

Slipping a finger inside, he curled it and found a spot that had me crying out. His name came out on a surprised groan.

"*Xander.*"

His finger slipped free and I felt empty. He lifted his head and looked up at me. His lips and beard glistened. Lifting his hand, he brushed his finger over my lower lip and coated it with my wetness.

"You are wet. Dripping. An aroused woman will coat a man's fingers, mouth and cock with her pussy juices." He pushed the tip of it past my lips and into my mouth. "Taste."

I tasted myself on my tongue as I sucked on it. Xander's eyes widened and his jaw clenched as I did so. He growled as he pulled his hand free.

"I want a taste," Mr. Tyler uttered.

Xander pushed to his feet and took hold of the bottom of my dress as the other man took his place between my legs.

Mr. Tyler took a moment and just looked his fill. "I can see her clit poking out from here. So easily aroused." Glancing up, he asked, "Do you want to come, baby?"

I wanted to do something, for I felt as if I was going

to burst out of my skin. My heart was racing and my skin flushed; the taste of myself was indeed sweet on my tongue.

I'd come before, not from Frank, but my own fingers late at night. Sometimes he wouldn't come home and I'd been able to explore my own body, to touch myself the way I liked. In all those moments, I'd never felt remotely like this.

"Yes," I whispered. "God, yes."

"I'm not God. Just Tyler. You're going to scream my name before I'm done with you."

Tyler pushed against the inside of my thigh, making me widen my stance. Only then did he lean in and put his mouth on me. Where Xander had been deliberate and aggressive, Tyler was focused and attentive. While he did pay special attention to my clit, he sucked one fold into his mouth, then the other before pushing the tip of his tongue inside me. I'd had Xander's fingers and Frank's member in me, but never a tongue. It wasn't big enough, nor did it go in deep enough to make me come, but the idea of Tyler filling me with his cock had me clenching his shoulders. I was lost, wild to the feelings.

These *men*. Lord above, these men were skilled. I had no idea what I'd been missing. I was in the entryway with my dress bunched about my waist with a man—a gorgeous man—between my legs doing wicked things to me! A second man stood by and watched. It was... wicked.

"You're going to come for Tyler, but not until I say," Xander whispered in my ear, the soft rasp of his beard on my neck another sensation to my already overwhelmed body.

How he knew I was almost on the brink, I didn't know. But with Tyler pressing his tongue flat against my clit as he dipped not one, but two fingers inside me, I didn't know how stop it.

I licked my dry lips as I gasped and cried out with pleasure. My eyes had fallen closed and I just gave in to the feeling.

"Not yet, Emily. Be a good girl and wait for your men to tell you when you can come. Your pleasure belongs to us now."

I turned my head to look at Xander, to tell him what he could do with his pushy ways. His face was right there. His dark eyes bored into mine, our breaths mingled.

"Stop."

I stilled at his order, but I realized when Tyler lifted his head and pulled his fingers from me that Xander was speaking to him, not me.

"No, don't listen to him. Don't stop!" I was panting now, as if I'd run the distance to Bridgewater instead of riding. I glanced down at Tyler—he, too, had slick lips—then at the fierce Xander.

"The next time you tell me I'm pushy, you'll be punished *and* you won't come," Xander vowed. "That's a promise."

Had I said those words aloud? It seemed Xander was not a man to be trifled with.

"You want to come so much, sweetheart, then you tell Tyler exactly what you want him to do." He stroked my hair back from my face with a gentleness that contradicted his tone.

"Make me come," I said. I'd never said these kinds of words aloud. Frank had never brought me pleasure before. In fact, I never knew it was actually possible with a man. Until now.

Out of the corner of my eye, I saw Xander shake his head. "How?" he asked.

Tyler wiped his mouth with the back of his hand. Waiting.

"How?" I repeated, confused.

"With my mouth?" Tyler asked.

"Yes."

"Then tell me you want to come on my mouth."

Tyler's hands gripped my thighs, his thumbs brushing along the crease, nudging the hairs of my pussy. My hips shifted of their own volition, wanting his fingers closer. On me. In me.

"I want to come on your mouth."

"With pleasure, baby. With pleasure." Tyler rewarded me with a grin just before he put his mouth back exactly where I wanted it.

"Oh, *yes*," I moaned.

"Do you want him to slip two fingers deep inside you?" Xander whispered in my ear. "Your pussy's so delectably tight, when you come you're going to squeeze them."

I did right then, just by the words alone.

My hips began to shift. I couldn't help it. I was close and I was chasing my pleasure, moving on Tyler's face so that I was closer... closer. Oh, so close.

"Yes, fingers. In me. Please."

I felt a hand on my bare bottom. "And what about here, sweetheart? Do you need a finger here, too?" As Xander spoke, a finger slipped between the seam of my bottom and over my...

"Xander!" I gasped. "You can't... oh, yes!"

He'd circled my back entrance, then slipped a slick fingertip into me. I'd never been touched there before, let alone have a finger work its way inside. The stretch was uncomfortable, but, it was dark and carnal and it felt so good.

"You have Tyler on his knees licking your clit, drinking down all your delectable juices. His fingers are filling your pussy while you have my finger in your ass. You like two men touching you. You like it when you have no choice but to take what we give you."

Xander kept talking, his dark words filling the remainder of my senses. I felt their hands everywhere. I could smell their unique scents and the heady aroma of my arousal. My lingering taste was on my tongue. I could see Tyler's head between my splayed thighs. I was overwhelmed, consumed.

"Please," I begged, my head thrashing against the door.

"Come, sweetheart."

I did. I obeyed Xander's command and came so blissfully hard I surely put marks on Tyler's shoulders with my fingernails. My scream filled the entryway and I could do nothing but clench and squeeze down on their invading fingers, riding the waves of pleasure that they gave me.

An arm banded about my waist and held me up, for my knees gave out and I would have collapsed to the floor.

Tyler stood to his full height and both men loomed over me. They, too, were breathing hard.

"We'd better get her to Olivia's before we fuck her,"

Tyler murmured. Putting his hand at the front of his pants, he adjusted himself. *Oh, my.* Through his pants, I could see the outline of his very large...

"I'd let you see my cock, baby, but then I'd have to fuck you."

I frowned, noting that both men's pants showed clear delineation of their desire.

"Don't you *want* to fuck me?" I asked, confused. "I thought... that was what I expected."

Xander took a step back. "Not until we're married, sweetheart. Then we'll fuck you and mark you and fill you with our seed."

3

TYLER

The day before...

"Just because you've found the men of your dreams does not mean you can play matchmaker," I told Olivia.

She gave me a look that was pure exasperation, especially when it was combined with a hand on her hip. My tiny cousin had three men wrapped around her little finger—husbands Cross, Rhys and Simon—and that was plenty. I did not need to be added to that list.

"Her husband *died*, Tyler," she countered. I glanced

at Rhys and Cross who flanked her, but I received no help from either of them.

"Why can't your men go with you?"

"Because you and Xander have nothing better to do. While you are just visitors here, we—" Rhys waved a hand between Cross and himself, "—live here and have been assigned the job of putting out tables."

"The picnic won't happen if we don't put out tables," Cross added.

I doubted that the church picnic would be cancelled if Olivia's husbands didn't *personally* put out the tables for the food. Surely there were other men—even other men from Bridgewater—who could complete the task. I did not wish to go to a ranch and drag a reluctant woman, a reluctant *widow*, to a church picnic.

"Do you really think she will come? She's just lost her husband, what, two days ago?"

A small boy ran between our little group and grabbed hold of Cross' legs. If he were a smaller man, he'd have been toppled by the force.

"Unca Cross!"

The big man beamed down at the two-year-old and swung him up into the air, tossing him high enough to make Olivia gasp. Christopher laughed and so Cross did it again.

"When we have children, you are *not* doing that."

Their Reluctant Bride

Olivia pursed her lips, but couldn't help but smile as Christopher called out, "Again!"

"Hurry back from getting Mrs. Woodhouse so we can get right on that," Rhys commented, giving my cousin a very heated gaze.

I turned my back on them and looked across the open field in front of the town's church for Xander. If I was going to retrieve a grieving widow, he was going with me. With the church service just ending, the townspeople were milling about, children playing tag or dipping their feet in the creek nearby. Women were organizing the food and sure enough, the Bridgewater men were moving tables in a long line for the food.

"There he is," Andrew said with a grin and a sigh. I stepped back to let the little boy's father join our group. "Your mother has your lunch, young man."

"Lunch!" he cried and reached out for his father, clearly eager to eat.

Watching the group from Bridgewater was inspiring. They embraced the same custom as my parents—two husbands for one wife. Olivia was my father's niece and she had *three* husbands. I, too, would take a wife with another. Xander. I saw him walking my way with Simon, who was looking solely at Olivia. I had no doubt Rhys' intentions upon our return from the widow's ranch. I knew with what they would occupy their time later:

baby making. How she hadn't become pregnant with three husbands before now was beyond me.

I frowned at the idea of my cousin being fucked by these men—any men—but they loved her and devoted their lives to her. It was a good thing Xander and I were staying elsewhere. Ian and Kane—who I'd sold cattle to the year before—and their wife, Emma, had gone to Billings and so we stayed in their house during our visit.

Bridgewater men needed privacy with their bride.

Olivia had said it had been like lightning when she'd first met her men. I knew of the concept, for my mother said the same thing. In fact, she'd been the one to give my cousin the notion. Love at first sight was fine for some, but I doubted it for me. Finding a woman wasn't easy, but finding a woman who would want two husbands was even harder. Especially Xander and me. Xander, the ex-convict and me, the... what was I? I loved women in general—there was nothing better than sinking into a hot pussy. Well, perhaps a tight little ass. But married to one? I wasn't sure if I was the kind of man that would dote on my bride the way Olivia's men doted on her.

She was the center of their world. I couldn't imagine ever finding a woman that would make me even consider it, let alone let the parson's noose slip around my neck. I could, though, be courteous and go with

Olivia to escort her friend to the picnic. My cousin was kind to think of the older woman.

"I understand I've been summoned," Xander said to the group at large.

A bell was rung indicating the start of the meal. People made their way from the blankets they'd spread out on the grass to the table laden with food.

"We are going with Olivia to retrieve a widow," I told Xander.

"Mrs. Woodhouse," Olivia added for Xander's benefit.

My friend looked between us, his dark eyes giving away none of his emotions. This was perfectly normal for him. I'd known him for five years and even I'd rarely seen him smile. The time in prison had changed him, hardened his emotions. "Are we allowed at least a chicken leg to take for the ride?" he asked, rubbing his stomach.

Olivia went up on her tiptoes and kissed Cross, while giving Rhys and Simon knowing looks. While she was married by Bridgewater standards to all three men, the townspeople only knew of her legal wedding to Cross. Public displays of affection were limited, but I had no doubt Olivia would make it up to the other two once home.

"Hurry back, wife. We have plans for you." I couldn't

miss Simon's murmur as we walked away and it confirmed my suspicions.

———

"Emily!" Olivia knocked on the door to the ranch house thirty minutes later. She shifted impatiently for her friend to answer the door.

Was she elderly and slow? Hard of hearing?

When Mrs. Woodhouse opened the door, I could definitively say no. She was close to Olivia's age, much too young to be a widow. She was petite and curvy and her modest dress did nothing to hide her very delightful curves. Her hair was the blackest I'd ever seen, yet her skin was as pale as cream. It was a striking contrast and I was mesmerized. While she offered Olivia a small smile, it was her eyes that showed pain and hurt. Her full mouth was pinched and dark smudges beneath her eyes made her look tired and worn down. Clear signs of her grief.

I removed my hat. "Ma'am, I'm sorry to hear about your loss," I replied.

Xander, who'd removed his hat before she'd even opened the door, offered a slight nod of his head.

"Thank you," she replied softly. Her voice was deep for a woman, smooth and silky.

Olivia stepped forward, wrapped an arm about her waist, and led her back inside. "We are here to take you to the picnic. Drag you if we have to."

Mrs. Woodhouse looked over her slim shoulder at us, wondering perhaps if we'd do just that.

I glanced at Xander. He just arched a dark brow, but said nothing.

Olivia laughed. "The fair-haired one is my cousin, Tyler, and the other one, the brooder—" she spun around and grinned impishly, "—is Xander."

We followed the women into the parlor. The room was clean, the fire unlit. Based on the size of the house and the quality of the furnishings, it would seem Mr. Woodhouse had been successful in his affairs.

"Gentlemen," she murmured as way of greeting, flicking her gaze up to us. "Olivia, I don't think I feel like going today. Perhaps another time."

Olivia shook her head. "We won't take no for an answer, will we?" She turned to glance our way and gave us a pointed look.

"No, we won't," I added. "It would be an honor if you'd let us escort you." She'd only said a few words, but I was intrigued. So was my cock. She was quiet and calm and beautiful and so damn constrained. I wanted to tug at the tight bun at the nape of her neck. I wanted to undo those prim buttons on her dress's snug collar. I wanted to bring color to her cheeks the only way I knew how, by making her come.

My cock swelled at the idea of mussing her up. The way Xander's gaze was fixed on her led me to believe he was thinking the same thing. It was wrong though, to have such thoughts about a woman who'd just lost her husband.

"Then it's settled. Go get your hat and we'll be off." Olivia was as good at pushing others around as she was her men.

Mrs. Woodhouse took a moment to consider, biting her plump lower lip as she did so.

"I do not have an offering for the picnic," she countered.

Olivia dispelled that worry with a wave of her hand. "There is plenty of food. You will not make anyone go hungry, I assure you."

Knowing arguing would do nothing when it came to Olivia, Emily finally offered a small nod and went through an open doorway toward the back of the house.

Once she was gone, Olivia spun on her heel and pointed to us as she whispered, "Be nice!"

I held up my hands in front of me in a defensive gesture. "That wasn't nice?" I whispered back.

"You." She pointed at Xander. "You have to say something. Talk. Have a conversation with the woman."

Their Reluctant Bride

Xander's mouth fell open slightly, but he said nothing.

I stifled a small smile and went to open the front door when Mrs. Woodhouse returned.

We helped the ladies into the wagon and I wondered why Olivia was so particular about us being nice to the woman. It wasn't until the ranch disappeared over a hill did I discover why.

"You know about the Bridgewater ways," Olivia said. She and Mrs. Woodhouse sat beside me on the wagon seat with Xander sitting at the back of the wagon, his lower legs dangling off the edge.

I glanced over at Olivia, surprised by her question. Their unusual customs were not well known and those from the ranch didn't share the information. Many would find it wrong, illegal even. My parents had been careful as well, especially since they lived in Helena, a large city in comparison to Bridgewater's open prairie. There was a reason she was speaking of it with Mrs. Woodhouse and I had a feeling I wasn't going to like the answer.

"Yes," Mrs. Woodhouse replied.

"Well, Tyler and Xander are looking for a wife."

No, I didn't like the answer at all. I pulled up on the reins and stopped the horse. "Olivia," I warned.

"Olivia, I'm not looking for—"

My cousin cut off the remainder of Mrs. Woodhouse's sentence. "Nonsense. Your husband was a brute. A tyrant and a drunk. You aren't mourning him and you need a husband."

To my surprise, Mrs. Woodhouse jumped down from the wagon and started to walk back toward her ranch. I gave Olivia a dark look, ready to chase after the woman, but Xander hopped off the back of the wagon instead.

He followed her, then ultimately caught up with her, but they continued to walk away from us.

I sighed. "Are you truly trying to play matchmaker?" I asked.

Olivia didn't look the least bit contrite and set her chin in an obstinate angle. "Yes. You need a wife and Emily is perfect."

"She's just lost her husband. How could she be perfect if she's clearly not interested?" I angled my head toward the direction she'd gone.

"Her husband gambled and drank to excess. While she never once confessed it, I believe he hit her. He was cruel to her at the very least. She is not the least bit sorry he's dead. In fact, if she weren't such a nice person, she'd be dancing on his grave."

The idea of anyone hurting Mrs. Woodhouse made my hands clench. She was too small, too... dainty—even with her lush curves—to protect herself from the likes of a man Olivia described.

"Then she can find a man she truly likes this time around. She's young, beautiful. She's a catch for any man in town."

Olivia grinned. "So you think she's beautiful?"

"Any conscious man would think so," I countered.

"Then you should offer for her."

I sighed, exasperated. "Why?"

"Because you and Xander need a wife."

I shook my head. "We do not *need* a wife."

"I see the way you look at the couples at Bridgewater. Everyone's happily married. It's hard, I'm sure, for you to witness since no one else marries like we do. Like your parents. You *want* a marriage with Xander like all of us at Bridgewater. Admit it."

"Of course, I admit it. I won't marry any other way." I put my hand up. "That does not mean that our bride should be Mrs. Woodhouse."

Olivia pursed her lips. "She has to marry."

My brows went up. "Again, why?"

"The bank is taking the ranch. Debts, most of them I'm sure are because of her husband's gambling. She has no place to go. No money. She'll have to get a job and there are none, unless she wants to work on her back."

"Olivia," I warned.

"What? It's true." Olivia took a deep breath. "She's going to have to marry. A woman doesn't have any other options. It might as well be you."

I frowned. "Is that a compliment?"

"Of course, it is. She deserves someone—or two someones—who will be good to her. I know you and Xander would be. Plus, I know her well and she knows about how we marry. I *like* her. Trust me, you'll be well suited."

I turned so I could look at the woman's retreating figure. Well suited? I had no doubt we'd be very compatible in bed. She would be no hardship to look at. That did not make a marriage, but it certainly helped.

4

Xander

It didn't matter to me that Olivia was matchmaking. I'd known her intention from the moment she asked us to escort her to claim her friend instead of her husbands. They would have done anything for the woman and the excuse of moving tables was a poor one. Laughable. There were enough strong backs at the picnic to complete the task instead of them. I was just pleased they were trusting enough of us to take her to the Woodhouse ranch. It wasn't as if we'd done anything to make them question our ability to protect their bride, especially with Tyler being family. To the contrary, in fact. They must consider us quite highly, but the Bridgewater men were a possessive and protective bunch.

Perhaps they were trying to take Mrs. Woodhouse under their wing. I'd heard that she'd been to the ranch before, knew of their ways and customs. The fact that she held that secret meant the men placed her in high regard. All this meant that it wasn't just Olivia that was trying to put Mrs. Woodhouse together with Tyler and me. The men were in on it as well and thought the woman was the one for us. Because of this, I'd been nothing less than curious about the widow.

When she'd opened the door, it had been difficult not to stare. Hell, she was a vision. It was her mouth I'd noticed first. Plump and full, it was a bright cherry pink, as if she'd been kissed all afternoon. It was when I met her gaze that I'd been intrigued. There, I saw a woman who'd seen hard times. She was exceptionally good at hiding it, but the stiffness of her shoulders and the tightness about those dark eyes were obvious indicators. I knew them well, for I saw hints of myself in her.

Not in her soft curves or the way her hips swayed as I walked beside her. Not in the long, slim column of her neck. Not in the pert turn of her nose. She may not have been wrongly convicted of a crime, but she'd been hurt. Had her husband been the sole culprit? Cruel parents?

She was too young for much more. Regardless, I felt a kindred spirit with this woman and I hadn't even said one word to her.

"You do not have to escort me any longer. I assure you, I know the way home." Her long dress swished against the grass.

Her short legs ate up the distance toward the ranch house and I slowed my gait to match hers.

"I am envious of you," I said.

Her head whipped around to look up at me, her eyes narrowed. "Envious? Of what, that my husband is dead? That my ranch is to be taken from me? That I have no place to go? That I am penniless?"

No wonder she looked wounded. She had a heavy burden to carry. She bit her lip as she most likely realized she'd revealed too much to a stranger.

"That Olivia is a friend who cares for you enough to play matchmaker."

She stumbled at my words and I grabbed her elbow to keep her upright. When I didn't release it, she eyed me suspiciously.

"Olivia is a good friend," she confirmed, squinting up at me in the bright sunshine.

I turned us so she would not face the glare.

"She and her husbands believe we should marry."

"You do not mince words," she countered.

"Bridgewater men know their woman on sight. If they believe we are well matched, then I believe it to be true."

She tilted her head and studied me. "What do *you* think?" Her deep voice prodded.

She was very perceptive. She was not being matched to any of the Bridgewater men, but to me and Tyler.

"I had not considered marriage—until about twenty minutes ago. I believe the men are all correct, that Olivia is correct."

"Oh?" she asked. I started to see her cool demeanor slip as I spoke.

"Lightning."

Her eyebrows went up and her mouth fell open. She knew to what I spoke, for Olivia must have explained it to her. It was how she'd felt when she met her men. It was how Tyler's mother described it, how he imagined it to be. Did Tyler feel it when he saw Emily? What I felt, it perhaps wasn't love at first sight, but the connection, the spark was palpable. It scared the hell out of me, for I was not a good match. I had dark places inside me, rough edges, a cool demeanor. I liked to fuck dark and rough. Surely Emily was too soft, too gentle to be handled in such a way.

"The topic is moot, for you have just lost your

husband. I would not dare intrude on your grieving for him. To take what you shared with him lightly."

I would never seek interest in another man's woman, even a man who was alive only in spirit.

She started laughing then. Turning, she began to walk back toward the house as she continued. I frowned, but fell in step beside her long enough to grab her arm and stop her.

As she wiped the tears from her cheeks, she said, "I do not mourn Frank. To the contrary. I am glad that he is dead. Unfortunately, his reach is strong from the grave."

The tone of her voice confirmed the truth of her words. It seemed they had not had a love match; that her tired and weary features weren't caused by mourning, but something else.

"He left you with nothing," I added, confirming her problems. Olivia was right, she had to wed. There was nothing else for her to do here in the Montana Territory. There were no appropriate jobs to be had. Even if she found a position as a laundress or even a house maid, she would have no protection, no man to keep her safe. The idea of her all alone left me cold inside.

She would be forced to leave town, to go to a larger city like Helena or Billings. But how would she make the journey? If the bank was to take the ranch, she would be left with the clothes on her back, no coins for food, let alone the stage. The burden she carried was heavy.

"That is true." She looked down, perhaps hoping to hide her feelings from me, and smoothed out her pale blue dress. "I do not know you, Mr. Xander, or Mr. Tyler either. I will not go from one bad marriage to another under the guise of *protection*. The protection I needed in my marriage to Frank was from Frank himself."

I couldn't argue with her, for she was correct. She didn't know me from Adam. Why would she want to shackle herself to two husbands when she hadn't even liked the one she'd had? Neither Tyler nor I were Frank Woodhouse, though. We wouldn't hurt her. While I would offer her the baser aspects of fucking—and being claimed by two men at once—she would always be given her pleasure. She would be cherished and sheltered, protected and possessed. We were the men for her and she would just have to come to discover that.

EMILY

As I helped the women collect dishes and plates, bowls and platters from the picnic tables and place them in baskets to be taken home, I tried to be involved in the conversations that swirled around me. While the women from town had always been wary of Frank, they'd never been fearful of me. They often veered away from us when we were together, but I had never been bothered by it, for I understood. With him gone, they had been nothing but kind throughout the picnic and I was glad I'd come. It was hard to keep up with the chatter as I kept an eye on the two men who had come to the house. I'd been coaxed back to the wagon and we rode to town in silence. Once Mr. Xander had lifted me and Olivia down from the seat, the men had tipped their hats and gone off to fill their plates. I hadn't spoken with them since. But, every time I looked their way, one of them was watching me. They weren't very subtle about it either. Often, I had both of them plus several of the Bridgewater men eyeing me. My cheeks heated every time and I turned away.

Their suggestion—even Olivia's matchmaking—was preposterous. They didn't know what went on in my house, what I'd endured, what I'd done. Surely, neither man would want me when they learned the truth. If the sheriff and the undertaker hadn't discovered it, then my secret went to the grave with Frank. That didn't settle my mind though or ease the guilt that I felt. The weight of my actions was heavy on my conscience.

Nor would either of the men want a woman who was penniless. My father had given Frank money to marry me—passed legally from one cruel man to another—and it had been lost at the gambling tables like water through a sieve. I had nothing to give either man except my body. No land, no house, not even any livestock. I wasn't a nubile eighteen-year-old and I most certainly wasn't a virgin. Wouldn't they want some sweet, innocent thing to be their bride? Looking around, I counted at least five eligible possibilities that were much prettier than myself. But, no.

I glanced at the men, who were leaning against one of the tables, metal cups in hand, drinking some of the beer that had been tapped from the cask that sat in the shady part of the creek. Their eyes were on me. One set fair, the other dark. Their gazes held heat and a promise of something very carnal. Was that what they wanted from me? Of course. Every man wanted to slake his needs in his wife's body. These two could have any woman they wanted, even pay for a saloon girl or two. They didn't need to wed anyone, let alone me. It was the why of it that I didn't understand.

"Mrs. Woodhouse."

A deep voice cut through my reverie and I broke the men's gazes.

Spinning on my heel, I was face to face with *him*.

Their Reluctant Bride

I took a step back, but he closed the distance. He'd said his name was Ralph when he'd come calling the other day. Frank had been buried only just that morning when he'd knocked on the door. He'd pushed his way into the house, knocking me back. The man was a brute. A bully. By the smell of him, he hadn't bathed in some time. His dark hair was greasy and matted where it stuck out from beneath his hat. He'd refused to remove it. While it showed his lack of manners in front of a lady, I hadn't needed that indicator. Nothing about him said gentleman.

"I offered you the time to *think* you had a choice, Mrs. Woodhouse."

I crinkled my nose at his foul breath. I retreated another step and this time he didn't follow. The soft breeze helped cut the stench of his powerful body odor.

"You will come to the back door of the saloon on Saturday night. You need not concern yourself with wardrobe, for I'm sure you will be outfitted with something more appropriate for your new role... or perhaps in nothing at all."

His eyes roved over my body and I felt dirty.

I shook my head. "I am not responsible for my husband's debts."

He grinned, showing off a gap in his lower line of teeth where a tooth should have been.

"He owes me five big ones. You'll pay it off or I'll tell the sheriff how your husband died."

My eyes widened and I felt all blood drain from my head. Dark spots flickered around the evil man's head.

I took a deep breath, trying to keep from fainting. I wasn't a fainter and I wouldn't start now. "How... what? I do not know to what you speak."

He chuckled and waggled his eyebrows. "I guess frying pans aren't just for cooking potatoes."

He knew. Oh, God, he'd seen me hit Frank. But how? It had been late at night. The house was dark. He couldn't know.

I waved my arms about the parlor. "Take what you want. Surely that clock or one of the horses should pay for my husband's debt. You don't need *me*."

He grinned, but it wasn't with any kind of warmth. His hand came up to touch me, but I stumbled backward. The grin didn't slip when he went over to the mantel and took the small clock, tucked it under his arm. "This," he tilted his head to indicate the clock, "is only to appease me since you've taken so long to decide. I don't want *things*, Mrs. Woodhouse. I want you. *You* will pay his debt. Come to town or I will drag you there by your hair."

"Mrs. Woodhouse, we've saved a piece of cherry pie for you."

Their Reluctant Bride

The voice pulled me from my thoughts. Woodenly, I turned and saw Mr. Tyler standing to my right. When had he approached? In his hand, he did indeed hold a slice of pie.

"Care to introduce me to your friend?" he asked, his voice deep. He eyed Ralph carefully.

5

Emily

Relief washed over me as if I'd been dunked in a cold creek. "No, I think not." I offered a smile, but was afraid that it was a tad brittle. "That pie looks wonderful. Thank you."

He held out his arm and I took it gladly, letting him lead me away.

I glanced over my shoulder and Ralph stood where we'd left him, eyeing me.

I turned away.

"Was that man bothering you?" Mr. Tyler asked.

With every step away from Ralph, the better I felt. I was so pleased to be away from the awful man I wanted to kiss Mr. Tyler for the rescue. Ralph, though, was my problem. What he knew was my problem. It was my secret to keep, my secret to solve. My father had given me to the first man who'd matched his ideas for a dutiful woman. I hadn't met them and Frank had treated me accordingly. He'd lost all our money, hadn't cared enough about me to keep me safe, to keep the ranch soluble. I could only rely on myself; that much I knew.

If Mr. Tyler found out the truth, he could even have me thrown in jail. I wouldn't go to prison after what Frank did to me so I would hold my secret safe.

"While I did not enjoy his company, he was not bothering me," I assured Mr. Tyler, making light of the situation.

Xander approached, but watched as Ralph walked off toward the center of town, most likely to the saloon.

"Is he our competition?" Xander asked, stroking his beard.

I couldn't help the laugh that escaped. The sudden burst of energy from the argument bled away and I felt weary. Ralph was *nothing* like the two men before me. He had a paunch and was overweight. Jowls hid the line of his neck. He was also ruthlessly cruel. Nothing about the man was appealing, not one greasy hair on his head.

Mr. Xander and Mr. Tyler, however, they were sheer perfection. Even with one being fair and the other dark, both of them were attractive to my feminine nature. They were tall and broad and brawny. Their size alone should have made them seem domineering and dangerous. Instead, they were dominant and powerful. I longed to be held in their arms, to be protected with their defined muscles.

"You do not need to fear of that," I told him.

The picnic was ending. Families were either walking home or riding in their wagons, small children napped on blankets in the back. No one was near us. I didn't even see the Bridgewater families any longer. The sun had moved across the sky, but it was still warm.

"Olivia had us tell you goodbye. Her men took her home with some haste after the meal."

I could infer what that meant and my cheeks flushed. I was pleased for my friend, that she had men so doting and so eager for her. I felt a pang of envy at what she had and what I'd longed for with Frank, but never had.

I gave a small nod in response, for what could I say?

"I hope you will accept our escort home," Xander added. By the tone of his voice and the way he didn't word it as a question, I had to assume he was just being courteous to allow me to even *think* I could deny them.

"You must know we wouldn't allow you to go the distance alone," Mr. Tyler added.

They were both gentlemen and while their presence was unnerving, it felt good to know they were concerned for me. I'd taken the route to town many times on my own. Frank hadn't cared.

"Very well."

"Xander told me about your conversation." I didn't know to what Tyler spoke. When I didn't reply, he continued. "About marrying us. You have my word—"

"Our word," Mr. Xander cut in.

"Our word, that no man would bother you again." He tilted his chin to indicate where I'd stood with Ralph.

I couldn't hold his gaze for I saw that he was earnest. Both of them were quite earnest in their words.

"You don't even know me!" I replied, stepping around him and walking away.

"I don't have to know you, I just have to *know*," Tyler called.

I shook my head and kept walking. I felt the truth of his words, for the men—crazily enough—called to something deep inside of me. I believed them when they said they'd protect me, and I could only imagine how it would feel to be sheltered in a man's embrace. In two men's holds.

I walked past the open field where the picnic had been held and headed south toward home. Well, home for the next few days before the man from the bank came to remove me. I heard their footsteps behind me.

"You're running because you're scared," Tyler said.

His words stopped me and I spun on my heel.

"Scared? You're damn right I'm scared!" I shouted, placing my hands on my hips.

Xander did as well, mimicking my stance. "Language like that should not come from your mouth. If you were mine, I'd spank you."

I narrowed my eyes at Xander. I was reacting to him on a visceral level. I wanted to strangle the man for being so presumptuous while my nipples tightened beneath my corset at the idea of him tossing me over his knee.

"Scared of *us*," Tyler clarified. "There's no reason to be scared of anything else. We'll protect you."

Protect me from Ralph? From being a whore? From jail or even worse, a noose around my neck?

Was that even possible? Could they save me? Protect me like a well-muscled shield against that evil man?

"We'd pleasure you, Emily." It was the first time either of them had used my given name. When Mr. Xander said it, it was like the rough tumble of rocks. Dark and deep as his personality.

My eyebrows went up. "Pleasure me? Like bring me

chocolates and such frivolous things? That's what you think I want?"

Xander stepped closer, his eyes on my mouth.

"I think you want to be fucked by two men who know what they're doing. Who will put your pleasure, your needs first. I think you want us to take all your worries away, to make that pretty little head of yours forget about your troubles. By the fire in your eyes, that might just be from a good bare bottom spanking."

My mouth fell open and my cheeks flamed at his words. "How dare you!"

"Emily, if there's one person in all of Montana Territory who needs to submit, it's you."

"Submit?" My heart beat so frantically against my chest I thought it might burst free. I was breathing hard and so unbelievably riled. These men had set me all a-dither. "I submitted to Frank for two years," I shouted. Tears blurred the men and I furiously wiped them away with my fingers. "If that's what you expect of a wife, then I want nothing to do with you."

"How we want you to submit is not the same thing at all, baby," Tyler said, taking a step closer. "Giving us your troubles, your body, your trust. That's submitting."

"Olivia submits to her men," Xander added.

Did she? I thought of my friend. Simon, Rhys and Cross wouldn't hurt a hair on her head. In fact, they'd protect her with their lives. She didn't appear cowed or belittled as a woman would who had to submit to her men.

"So do the other women," Tyler continued. "Laurel, Emma, Rebecca. The others, too. Do you think they're unhappy?"

They were the happiest women I knew. At the ranch, I saw the easy affection; holding hands, a brush of knuckles down a cheek, an easy kiss. I was so confused. I didn't understand this type of submission, for I'd only known subservience and misery. I hadn't been cherished, hadn't felt a soft caress of Frank's hand. He'd barely even kissed me. These men, they were offering things, expecting things from me I didn't even understand. They were overwhelming!

"You may have submitted to your husband, Emily, but he didn't give you what you deserved in return. We will show you how it should be. *Will* be. We'll do things to your body you never even imagined. You give us what we want and we'll give you exactly what you need."

"By the confused look on your face, I'll clarify," Xander said. "We'll fuck you. Your pussy, your mouth. Your ass. I bet your nipples are a pretty pink, tight right now inside that stiff corset. I like pinching them, tugging on them. I won't be gentle, Emily. I can't, but I swear you'll love it."

My mouth fell open at Xander's very explicit words. My nipples *were* hard as he'd said. I liked the idea behind his dark words and that made me... crazy. It was madness that I was aroused by such talk.

"We'll take you together, Emily," Tyler added. They were surrounding me, bombarding me with mental images, thoughts so fast I couldn't keep up. "You'll be surrounded, overwhelmed, taken."

"I can't... it's too much. *You're* too much." I turned and continued on. How could I think clearly when they were so... big? So virile. God, I wanted what they'd said. To be safely between them knowing I'd be taken care of. What would it be like to not have a care in the world, to be safe from the likes of Ralph or not legally wed to a brute like Frank? I doubted I'd have to touch myself alone in bed at night ever again if I married them.

"Do you want us to bring the wagon or do you wish to walk?" Tyler asked, still following but not too closely. I was surprised by his question, for it was completely a different topic, but I was pleased he hadn't continued the heated line of conversation.

"Walk," I replied. And so I did. I walked the path to the house once again, but this time I had two men behind me the whole way. They didn't say anything further until the house came into view.

"We'll watch you from here," Tyler said.

I turned. They were brightly lit with the setting sun. Little crinkles were at the corners of their eyes as they squinted.

"Thank you for escorting me home." Good manners dictated the response.

"We want to marry you, Emily. We want you to be ours. We'll give you some time to think about it. To decide. You know where to find us, if you need anything."

Tyler's voice was calm, but his intent was serious.

"Lightning, Emily," Xander said.

Tyler nodded and smiled. "Exactly. It's just like lightning."

I didn't answer, just turned on my heel and walked the rest of the way to the house. I had thinking to do. Plenty of it, and I feared my thoughts would be filled with those dominant men instead of how I was going to handle Ralph.

6

Emily

"Don't hide from me! I will find you and when I do, I'll tan a stripe off your hide, then you're going to do your wife's duty."

The way he slurred his words and stumbled about, I knew Frank was drunk. Again. When he was sober he ignored me, but when he came home full of rotgut whiskey and angry for losing even more money playing cards, he was downright mean.

He'd hit me only a few times, but more often than not, he'd come in late, drunk and eager to slake his desires with my body. I didn't want him on top of me again, smelling of cigar smoke, cheap perfume the saloon girls wore and like the bottom of a whiskey bottle. He stumbled up the steps, swearing as he went.

I gripped the frying pan as I stood in the bedroom, waiting.

I wouldn't hide, nor would I let him touch me. No more.

I saw his dark form in the hallway. It was a clear night and the moon shone brightly through the windows.

"There you are," he barked. "Where the hell's the money? It's not in the jar in the kitchen."

I stiffened my spine as I took a step toward him. The fact that he was more interested in gambling away our money instead of bedding me was telling. He was most certainly desperate. The frying pan was at my side and he'd yet to see it. It wasn't the best weapon, but he'd taken the rifle with him into town. I had nothing else for protection besides the pan I used to cook him breakfast.

"I hid it," I replied. I tried to hide the quaver in my voice, although he was probably too liquored up to hear it anyway.

"I owe Ralph that money. You go get it right now!" He waved his arms about.

I startled, but held my ground. I swallowed, then took a deep breath. "No."

It was the first time I'd outright refused him. That money was for food, not to be lost in a game of cards.

"What did you just say?" Even in the dark I saw the dark gleam to his eye. "Why, you little—"

I screamed as he came toward me, his arm up, fist clenched and ready to strike. I was ready, too.

I dodged to the side and swung the pan with all my might. It made contact, hard, and I shuddered. The sound of a sickening crack filled the quiet night.

He slumped to the floor and I stood above his form. He wasn't moving. He wasn't breathing—I couldn't hear his usual sluggish wheeze. I dropped the frying pan. It hit the floor with a loud thunk beside my bare feet.

I ran into the bedroom and lit the lamp, carrying it back into the hallway. Dropping to my knees, I couldn't miss the way the side of his skull was bashed in. His eyes, so filled with hatred these past few months, stared blankly straight ahead.

I couldn't leave him there. The sheriff would know. No one fell down and crushed the side of their head. I had to make it look like an accident, as if he were drunk and fell. The stairs! I pushed him, then recoiled back, at first afraid he would jump up and hit me. No. His eyes were vacant. He was definitely dead. Wincing, I pushed him closer to the stairs. His dead weight—I gagged once, thinking about what I'd done—made the work hard. By the time I had him precariously close to the top step, I was sweating in my nightgown. Resolute, I pushed with a deep groan. Down he tumbled, hitting step by step until he landed in a heap at the bottom.

Bile rose to my throat as I looked down at my dead husband. What had I done? I grabbed the lantern and ran for the bedroom, slammed the door shut.

I jerked awake with a gasp. Frank wasn't here. He wasn't coming after me. He was dead and buried and I was safe, at least from him. My nightgown was wrapped around me, my skin coated with a cold sweat. I took deep breaths to calm my racing heart. I *was* safe. I was alone in the house. I shuddered once, twice, remembering the feel of his dead body as I pushed him down the stairs.

Settling myself, I laid back down, pulled the covers up. Sleep wouldn't come now. I tried to push away the knowledge that I'd killed my husband. It didn't matter now. Everyone believed the tale I'd told. Why would they think other than what I'd said? Frank was a drunk. Everyone in town knew it. If he fell down the stairs after a night of hard drinking and gambling, who was going to doubt me? The sheriff himself had inspected the body and given me the death certificate with barely a question.

Except Ralph knew the truth. I didn't know how, but

he did. The fear returned, that gnawing worry in my belly. Perhaps he was bluffing, but it didn't matter. I couldn't risk it. Frank had left me penniless and Ralph was after me for more. I'd offered him anything he wanted from the property; it all belonged to the ranch anyway. He only took the clock to show his power over me, but he wouldn't relent. He knew it and still expected me to whore myself in trade.

Frank was as little help to me dead as he was alive. At least with him gone, I didn't have to worry about him coming home drunk and wanting to use my body. I didn't have to worry about him stealing the food money to gamble away. I'd been saddled to the miserable man for years. Unless I solved the problem about Ralph, I wouldn't be truly free. He expected payment and come Saturday, I'd be his.

I thought of the families at Bridgewater. Olivia was married to three men. Three! Simon, Cross and Rhys were *nothing* like Frank. They were kind and caring and confident and they doted and loved on Olivia as if the sun and moon circled about her. They were also very protective and... dominant toward her, but she did not seem to shy away from that as I had from Frank. Just as Mr. Tyler and Mr. Xander had said, she submitted to them.

Did I want to submit to those two men? They offered marriage and all the promises that went with it. But did I want to marry them and let them be controlling and dominant and in charge? Would they be like Frank or like Olivia's husbands? The possibility of those two taking away my burdens was powerful. I'd been a good wife, a dutiful wife to Frank, but he hadn't been a worthy husband. Had that been the problem? Had Frank been the problem? Would they ease my concerns? Could they protect me from Ralph?

Of course, they could. I sat up in bed once again, listened to the soft sounds of the night. The men were my only option. If I married them, Ralph would have to leave me alone, to give up. He wouldn't want to fight Mr. Tyler or Mr. Xander. There was no competition there. I knew from Olivia that they ran a cattle ranch over a day's ride from Bridgewater. If I married them, perhaps Ralph wouldn't even know where I'd gone. The men could literally take me away from my problems.

The price, however, would be my freedom. My body. My life. I'd have to give over to them in everything. They'd told me so in very carnal detail. They wanted to *fuck* me. Just the thought had my body warming. I pushed the sheet off my legs. What would it be like to have two men? Could I handle it? If Olivia could satisfy three men, surely I could meet two men's needs. Couldn't I? I wasn't a virgin, or young. I didn't know the first thing about any of the carnal things they'd mentioned. What if I wasn't enough? What if I couldn't please them?

I groaned. I was thinking in circles. The solution to my problems had stood before me. Two tall, handsome, powerful men. My bedroom abilities were the least of my concerns. I'd wasted an entire day thinking about them. Had they changed their minds? What if they'd found another woman who'd struck their fancy on their way back to town? Were they that dishonorable? I panicked at the possibility. Nothing could happen now in the middle of the night. There was nothing to do except wait until morning, put on my best dress and ride to Bridgewater and find out.

XANDER

I couldn't believe she'd knocked on the door and agreed to marry us. She'd ridden to Bridgewater, to Kane and Ian's house, specifically wanting us. Not to visit Olivia.

When I'd come down the stairs and saw her standing there, heard the words, "I'll fuck both of you," from her lips, I'd been stunned. While I'd longed to hear a woman say those words, I'd never expected it to happen. It was hot as hell and absolutely scary.

Tyler had grown up knowing he had two fathers, that they married and shared his mother together. The dynamic of it was a way of life for him. I'd met all three of his parents and saw how well it worked, how the two men loved Tyler's mother. They doted on her. Cherished her. Protected her.

I wasn't worthy of a wife of my own, my background being shit. What woman—even a desperate widow—would want a convict for a spouse? I hadn't had one parent, let alone three like Tyler.

But I wanted her and I'd told her as much. It didn't mean that I would be good for her. I'd been selfish in my words, but I didn't want any other man but Tyler and me to have her.

I felt better knowing that any bride I had would also have Tyler. Tyler's customs—Bridgewater customs—protected Emily from me, from my past. If anything happened to me, she would be safe with Tyler.

After we left her the day before, I figured Tyler and I would have to woo her, perhaps even remain at

Bridgewater for the appropriate length of time and court her. How the hell that was done, I had no idea. I could only hope that Tyler knew what to do. The direct approach hadn't worked, for we'd watched her stomp off, all riled up from our conversation, and not in a good way. I'd probably fuck up a simple courtship since I wasn't the wooing type. I'd told her straight out what we'd do to her and I feared I'd pushed it too far. I had been honest though. She'd known exactly what we were like.

But when she'd stood in the entryway, pretty as a picture and said she'd fuck us both, I almost came then and there in my pants. Between the two of us, I wasn't the gentle one. I wouldn't hurt Emily, no way in hell, but the darkness inside of me made me stern. Rough. Demanding. I was overwhelming and possibly even scary to someone as innocent and... fragile as Emily.

I'd lost control of my life when I'd been sent to jail. Now that I was free, I held that power in a tight grasp and refused to give it up to anyone, even a little slip of a woman. So when I'd pushed Emily up against the front door, dropped to my knees, stripped off her drawers and ate her sweet pussy, she knew right away that I wouldn't be a tender lover.

When Tyler had taken his turn, it was the sight of

her submitting so sweetly to his touch—she hadn't even known she'd done it—that had me savoring the taste of her on my tongue. She'd come so beautifully, so completely, for him.

"Fuck," I murmured, saddling up for the trip to town to get the sheriff. As justice of the peace, he'd seen to a Bridgewater wedding before and was familiar with the haste. "We need to hurry."

I couldn't wait to get back and have Tyler say the words. Make her legally his. She'd be mine as well. Just because the laws didn't allow for two men to share a bride, it didn't mean my honor wouldn't commit me to her just as seriously.

"I know. Jesus," Tyler replied. He ran a hand over the back of his neck and shook his head.

It wasn't a surprise she'd agreed to marry Tyler. He was a man any woman could want. He was rich, powerful in the Montana Territory and ran a successful cattle business started by his two fathers. Women turned their heads in his direction as they passed and he was a skilled lover. The way he'd made Emily come was proof enough.

I shifted my cock to a more comfortable position as we mounted up, thinking about her face when she'd come. Emily had agreed to go visit Olivia while we went to town. She hadn't been bothered by our haste and had been adamant the ceremony occurred at Bridgewater. In fact, she wanted the legalities done as quickly as we did. Had her orgasm made her so eager for more?

"She said yes," I said, surprise coating my words. I turned the horse toward town and squeezed my thighs to get the horse into motion.

Tyler turned his head and grinned. He rode up beside me. "She said yes. I can still taste her."

She tasted sweet, like honey, but musky and almost decadent. She was like the finest whiskey; I wanted more.

"You should have seen her face when she came. She's so fucking beautiful."

Tyler groaned. "I don't think her husband took care of her."

I shook my head. There was no way that man pleasured her in bed. The way she responded to us, so easily and with such surprise, it was as if she'd never come for a man before. If that were the case, she now had a hint of what it would be like later, after the short ceremony.

Good thing her asshole husband was dead, for I'd kill him all over again. I didn't care if I went back to jail. Emily didn't deserve to be with a drunk who didn't treat her well. She deserved orgasms every day from her men.

"She'd been surprised that we would take her up against the wall."

"Or during the daytime."

"Or with our mouths."

My cock was hard again. Fuck. I spurred my horse to a faster pace. "We have much to teach her. Tonight."

7

EMILY

Tyler and Xander had escorted me to Olivia's house, but allowed me to go to the door on my own. They were eager to go to town and return with the sheriff to perform the ceremony. When I'd said yes to marrying them, I hadn't expected it to happen immediately. But after what they'd done to me—God, I still felt the aftereffects of their attentions—perhaps it was a good idea. I wore no drawers, Xander had tucked them somewhere I couldn't find, and I was wet between my thighs. Sensitive. Achy.

A quick marriage was a good thing, but not in town. I hadn't wanted to return there for it. What if Ralph saw me? What if he told the men of what I'd done? They wouldn't marry me then and surely the sheriff would toss me directly into the jail cell. What man would want to marry a killer? If they didn't marry me, I didn't know what I'd do. Damn Frank. He might even ruin what could be between Tyler, Xander and me. The way my... pussy tingled, I had a fair idea of what that might entail.

They offered up a gentle stroke of fingers down my cheek before going to saddle their horses in the stable. I took a few moments to myself, the two of them overwhelming not only my body, but my thoughts as well. I lingered outside of Olivia's house in the bright sunshine, thinking. About them.

I'd worried they wouldn't want me, but that had been for nothing. They hadn't just agreed, they'd taken over. They'd been controlling and bossy and had made good on their word about how they would take me. I'd thought after we'd marry, not right then up against the front door. My... pussy contracted at the memory of their mouths on me there. I had no idea that was even possible, or that a man could put his finger in my bottom, as Xander had done. Oh, it had all felt so good. Everything they'd done had been... incredible.

They'd had hard cocks, and had been unsatisfied after seeing to me. I'd thought they would fuck me then, but they had refused, saying fucking was for marriage. I'd been surprised by their vehemence of this, but it told of their honor. After the ceremony though, I would have two very eager, very randy husbands to please.

A sound distracted me from my thoughts. Another. I looked toward the house when I heard a woman cry out. Olivia. It was a shrill, painful sound. I knew it well, for Frank had hit me and the sound had escaped my own lips a time or two. Olivia's men were hitting her? That had to be wrong. They wouldn't do that. I paused. Would they?

I bit my lip, deciding. I only had Frank as an example of a husband and so it was certainly possible.

I would not allow my friend to be abused by her husbands. I'd allowed Frank to be miserable to me for years before I'd had enough. But I'd only had one man to contend with. Olivia couldn't hit three men over the head with a frying pan and get away with it. Walking quietly up the steps to the front door, I opened it and listened. A ticking clock, the sound of the warm wind behind me was all I heard. Had I been mistaken?

"No, I don't want that," Olivia said, her voice drifting softly down the hall.

"You will." One of her husband's voices was deep and commanding, although quiet. They were in the men's office at the back of the house.

A loud crack filled the air, making me jump. Olivia cried out. "No!"

They *were* hitting her!

"We know what you need." Another voice.

"I don't need *that*," Olivia countered.

Another hit.

I couldn't stand by and let them hurt my friend. I didn't care that the men were bigger than me.

I grabbed the rifle that was on pegs by the front door, loaded and ready for any kind of danger outside. It was good enough for trouble inside as well. The heavy weight of it made my arms drop to my sides but I lifted it, walked down the hall and barged into the library.

"Leave Olivia alone!" I shouted, swinging the gun.

I skidded to a stop just inside the doorway as I took in the scene before me. Olivia was naked and bent over one of the desks. Simon's hand was stroking over the reddened skin of her bottom as Cross had two of his fingers deep inside her... oh, my. They weren't in her pussy, but in her back entrance, like Xander had done to me earlier. But Cross was using two fingers and they were *all* the way inside of her.

Oh, dear God! The area that he had stretched open was slick and shiny. Her woman's core was bare of any hair and I could see the lips there were bright pink and swollen and equally glistening. Rhys held a strangely shaped piece of wood near Olivia's lowered head. In his other hand was his... oh, my, his member and it was big and red and very large. He was stroking it slowly with his fist. I'd never seen one so big. Well, I'd only seen Frank's and it had been nothing like that. The outlines of Xander and Tyler's cocks indicated they would be comparable in size. I swallowed at the idea of something that big fitting inside me. Xander had even said he wanted to put it in my... ass. I clenched down at the thought.

Rhys and Cross froze at my surprised appearance. Simon turned to face me. His own member was sticking out from his open pants and I couldn't help but stare. Actually, I didn't know quite where to look.

"Emily!" Olivia cried out. This time the sound of her voice held a hint of embarrassment, not fear.

"Emily, put the gun down," Simon said, holding his hands out in front of him. I didn't know if I should stand my ground on the off chance that they were hurting Olivia—clearly they weren't—or run away embarrassed.

I felt my cheeks heat and I turned away, lowered the gun. "I'm... I thought you were hurting her."

I wished the earth would swallow me up in this moment. They were touching Olivia intimately, doing wicked, dark things to her. I dashed out of the room and, with fumbling fingers, put the rifle back on the wall in the entry. My arms ached from holding the heavy weapon.

Simon's large frame filled the doorway. "Emily, we would never hurt her. You must know that."

I nodded, but couldn't look him in the eye. "Yes, I know."

"You've been married, but you will learn, things are done differently here at Bridgewater. Xander and Tyler will show you."

I didn't admit to him that they already had, at least a little bit.

Although I couldn't see Olivia, I heard her breathy moan. Her other men didn't stop their attentions because of my interruption.

"Hear that? We aren't hurting her, but pleasing her. She likes it, likes what we do with her, even though it may have sounded otherwise."

"Yes, all right." I just wanted to say whatever it took to make a hasty retreat.

"I assume, since you're here, that you've agreed to marry?"

I nodded, looking at the floor.

"Where are your men?" he asked.

Olivia groaned. "It's so big."

I flushed again, guessing of what she spoke. "They are to bring back the sheriff. I will... um... wait at their house, I mean, at Ian and Kane's house for them. I'll let you... um... get back to Olivia."

I didn't wait for him to say anything more, but dashed out the open doorway and down the steps.

"Yes! More, Rhys. Please, more!" Olivia's very satisfied voice drifted to me, even as I ran away.

TYLER

"Simon said we should ask you after an encounter you witnessed while we were in town," I said, closing the door to Ian and Kane's house behind us. It was the door that we'd pressed Emily against only hours ago, all of us discovering just what it would be like between us. She was our bride now, the sheriff happily coming to Bridgewater to perform the quick service.

"What did you see, sweetheart?" Xander asked, hanging up his hat on the peg.

She wouldn't meet either of our eyes and her hands fidgeted with her dress. I had a good idea what she'd come upon, but I wanted to hear it from her. I was enjoying how flustered she was. It was a clear sign that while she'd been married, her dead husband hadn't stolen all of her innocence.

"Oh, um... well, I interrupted them."

Bridgewater men didn't just copulate with their wives under the cover of darkness, pushing up their bride's nightgown to rut. They possessed her body and soul. Nothing was considered inappropriate. Ass training and fucking. Cock sucking. Two men at once, filling both holes. Nipple play. If a Bridgewater woman was needy, their men took care of her, whenever. Wherever.

"Were they fucking?" Xander asked, trying to coax the words from her.

Her head whipped up and her mouth fell open. Her cheeks turned a bright shade of pink. "Well, no. Not exactly."

"Were they licking her pussy?" I asked. Her dark eyes met mine and I watched as her pupils dilated. Ah, she liked dirty talk, but was unused to it.

She shook her head and bit her lower lip.

I reached into the small cloth bag Rhys had given me. A wedding present, he'd said, then slapped me resoundingly on the shoulder. It was full of the handmade dildos and plugs he'd lathed. It was a hobby of his and came in quite useful for everyone at Bridgewater. Bridgewater men liked to train their women for ass play and ass fucking and so would Xander and I.

"Were they using something like this?" I held up a plug that would soon fill Emily's virgin ass. We'd take her there, fuck her together eventually, Xander filling that untried hole while I took her tight pussy.

Her eyes widened at the sight of it. It wasn't the smallest plug, for it wasn't slim or short. In fact, when we worked this inside of Emily she'd have a very good idea of what a cock there would feel like.

"They weren't... not yet."

Xander walked off into the parlor and I held out my arm to direct her to follow. There, Xander sat down in one of the comfortable chairs situated around the cold fireplace.

"So they weren't fucking her and she didn't have a plug in her ass," Xander commented. "That means they were preparing her for the plug, for fucking her there. Who had his fingers in your friend's ass?"

Xander was much more blunt than me.

"Cross," Emily admitted.

His directness worked with our new bride, for I was surprised she'd actually respond. But she had. That meant she'd respond to other things Xander said. I arched a brow and eyed Xander as I offered a slight nod. I wanted him to continue.

"Take off your dress, sweetheart." Xander placed his elbows on the armrests and steepled his fingers together, intent on watching.

Her pink lips fell open and I heard a little gasp escape. The sound went right to my cock. I wanted to see those lips parted and stretching around the blunt head.

"Do you need my help?" I came up behind her and kissed her nape. She startled. "Shh," I crooned against her sweet-smelling skin. It was soft as silk and warm beneath my lips.

"Xander's the bossy one. Let's show him what he wants." I tossed him the plug so I could have both hands free. Reaching around, I slowly undid the button at the top of her modest dress. I knew she had no drawers beneath, for we hadn't given them back earlier.

I watched as her breathing changed, how her breasts rose and fell against my hands as I worked my way down the front. As I looked over her shoulder, I could see the creamy expanse of her breasts thrust up above her snug corset. Her shift did nothing to hide how enticing they were.

Once the buttons were complete, I placed my hands on her slim shoulders, gently and carefully as not to scare her. I didn't think she would bolt like a skittish horse, but if I were to have my cock inside of her anytime soon, I wanted her amenable. Slowly, I slid the dress off her shoulders and down her arms, lower and lower it went until it was caught about her waist. With one last push and a slide of my hands around her lush curves, it fell silently to the floor.

A muscle in Xander's neck pulsed at the sight of her.

Working my hands back up her hips, I lifted the delicate material of her shift as they went. Little by little, her pussy became exposed to Xander's gaze. He leaned forward, placing his forearms on his thighs and sucking in a breath.

I didn't stop my upward motion until the shift was free of her hair and I dropped it to the floor. Wanting to see her, I came around from behind her and looked my fill.

Emily stood before us, nervous as hell, yet remaining still. Her corset squeezed her waist tightly, which only lifted and plumped up her full breasts. If the top didn't have lace edging then her nipples would surely be visible.

Her pussy, hell, her pussy was stunning. Pink lips couldn't be hidden by dark curls. Her clit poked out, as if eager for our mouths again. Once we shaved her bare, nothing would hide her beauty. My cock pressed painfully against my pants, eager to feel her slick heat.

"You're stunning, sweetheart." Xander's voice was

softer than I'd ever heard it. He crooked a finger and she took a tentative step closer, then another until she stood between his spread knees. He cupped her ass and stroked that supple skin before reaching up and unhooking the stays of her corset. When he let the stiff garment fall to the floor, her breasts spilled free.

Xander swore beneath his breath as he cupped them in his palms. They were full to overflowing and the nipples, a lovely blush color, tightened.

I itched to touch her. She was ours now. Nothing prevented me from doing so, so I came up behind her, pressed the length of my body against her back. I knew when she cried out that she'd felt my cock at her lower back. When Xander slid his hands down her belly and between her legs, widening her stance so he could stroke over her sensitive flesh, I took my turn to cup her breasts.

They were more than a handful, teardrop-shaped and heavy in my palms. With a flick of my thumbs, her nipples tightened even further. When I tugged at the tips, she arched her back and cried out.

"It's different with two men, isn't it?" I murmured, enjoying myself. I could play with her breasts all day as Xander did other things to her. I wasn't alone in seeing to her pleasure.

She nodded against my shoulder. "Frank, he never... it was never like this." Her voice was breathy, stunned.

I knew when Xander slipped a finger inside her, for she went up on her toes, which made her nipples pull taut between my fingers.

"She's dripping wet," Xander commented, his head lowered and watching his hand at work. "And squeezing my fingers. I can't wait to get her on my cock."

A little moan escaped her lips when he slipped his fingers from her, opened his pants and his cock fell free. A rare grin split his face when he looked up at Emily as he stroked it.

"This is for you, sweetheart. Climb on and go for a ride."

I was glad Xander didn't want to draw this out. I'd been ready for her since I opened the door to her earlier. He'd checked her for readiness. By the wet sound that was made when Xander had pulled his fingers from her pussy, I knew she was well primed for our cocks.

With my hands on her hips, I helped Emily settle her knees on either side of Xander's hips, then lowered her onto the broad head of his cock.

When she sank down, little by little, filling her pussy with his big cock, she reached up and gripped his shoulders for balance. Her eyes widened and her mouth opened in utter surprise.

She shook her head and began to squirm in his lap. "It's too big. No... this won't work."

Running a hand down the length of her spine, I tried to soothe her. "Shh, baby. He'll fit. I promise. Take it slow. Nice and slow and let him in."

The sooner she rode Xander to completion, the sooner I could find my own release.

8

Emily

He was too big. God, Xander's... cock was much too large to fit inside me. Frank had been small in comparison to Simon's and Rhys' cocks I'd seen inadvertently earlier, but Xander...

His cock was thick and long with a plum-colored head. Thick veins ran up the length of it when he'd gripped the base. It was stretching me open, stretching me wide... so wide I squirmed and tried to lift myself off, but Tyler held my hips still and was working me lower and lower.

I clawed at Xander's shoulders, frightened. "I don't want it."

Tyler's hands disappeared and Xander's big hand cupped my jaw. It was so warm and I could feel the rough calluses on his palm. "Stop moving," he commanded.

I stilled, with only part of him filling me. The bite of his words gave me focus, something to pay attention to other than my fear.

"Good girl. Now, just settle. That's it. You're so wet, sweetheart, my cock head is coated. Take a deep breath and relax. That's right."

Xander's tone, while direct, was almost soothing. He was directing me, distracting me from the discomfort. When I did relax my inner walls, I slipped a little bit lower on him. He was right, my wetness eased his entry, but I still felt as if I were being split open.

"Lift and lower yourself, get used to the feel of my nice, big cock."

I came up onto my knees and pulled up off of him, but the flared head was notched just inside me, caught within me by my swollen pussy lips. Carefully, I lowered back down just a touch. Up and down I went, just a fraction of an inch, then more until the wet sounds of fucking filled the air.

"I love seeing her pussy swallow up your cock," Tyler murmured. "And the way her breasts are bouncing, God, I'm going to come before I even get inside her." I hadn't realized until then my eyes had fallen shut and I'd almost forgotten he was there. I'd forgotten everything but the feel of Xander cramming into me. There wasn't a better word for it, because with every little bit of entry he gained, the fit was so tight. When I finally sat directly on his denim-clad lap, the feel of it rough against the backs of my thighs, I opened my eyes.

Xander was watching me, his eyes almost black, his jaw clenched tight. The corner of his mouth ticked up. "See, sweetheart, a perfect fit." His hands came to my hips. "Time to move now. Ah, shit, don't squeeze my cock like that unless you want me to come right now."

He growled when I did it again and I realized my feminine power. That was short-lived, for his grip tightened and he began to move me as he wished until I was truly riding his cock. The burn and the stretching were replaced with intense waves of pleasure, especially when Xander brought his hips up as he pulled me down onto him. The slight bite of pain as he hit the end of my channel morphed into delicious pleasure.

Somehow, his cock stroked over places inside I had no idea even existed, and that made me hotter and even eager for more.

"Yes," I gasped, on one rough thrust. I gripped his shirt, clawed at his shoulders as I let my head fall back, my hips beginning to move of their own accord, circling and moving to build the pleasure. To follow it.

Hands cupped my breasts as I continued to move, fingers plucking at the nipples. On one sharp pinch, I cried out.

"She likes it," Tyler commented. He pinched a little harder.

"Jesus, she's squeezing my cock when you do that. Again," Xander replied.

Tyler tugged this time, pulling on my nipples so that as I moved they were stretched painfully taut.

I couldn't stand it. It was too much. *They* were too much. I came on a gasp, then I screamed as Xander picked up the pace, using my body to stroke his cock, to coat him with my arousal and bring him to his own completion.

I was lost, completely oblivious to anything but the feelings these two men could wring from my body. It was hot and soft and painful and so amazingly incredible that I never wanted it to end.

I felt Xander's grip on my hips tighten even further as he thrust once, twice more, then buried himself within me. He groaned as I felt him pulse, filling me with his seed, coating me with the hot fluid.

Our ragged breathing mingled and I slumped against his chest. I heard his heart beat wildly beneath my ear. I didn't know how long we remained like that, but when Xander lifted me up and off his cock, I hissed at the slow slide and the hot gush of seed that followed. Sitting up, I looked at him and bit my lip.

"I'm sorry I—"

He put a finger over my lips. "Shh. Never say you're sorry about anything when we're fucking. It's natural. It's perfect. We need to know how you feel, how it feels when we touch you, fill you up. Work your body. We will push you, Emily. That's in my nature. In Tyler's."

"I was afraid," I admitted. "I was... overwhelmed."

"We *are* overwhelming," he commented, and I smiled. "It's Tyler's turn, sweetheart. You don't want him to die of blue balls, do you?"

I frowned at the question and glanced over my shoulder.

Tyler had his cock out and was stroking it. I watched as a bead of fluid seeped from the slit and dripped down the flared head. His cock was longer than Xander's but not quite as thick. My inner walls clenched at being filled by his as well. I knew I could take it now.

"Up onto your knees. Higher. Good. Now stick your ass out and show me that pussy."

I followed his instructions and it put my breasts directly in Xander's face. My bottom was thrust out toward Tyler and I was in a most wanton position. No doubt he could see Xander's seed slipping from me, for I felt it work its way down my thighs.

"I'm going to suck on these sensitive nipples as he fucks you." Xander seemed very eager by the idea. When he leaned in and did just that, I gasped, then relaxed into the warm, wet suction.

Tyler stroked a finger over my folds. "Swollen and dripping with Xander's seed. I can't tell you what it does to me seeing your slit like this. It's my turn to mark you, baby."

He took the step that separated us and lined his cock up, sliding it through my wetness, then notching it at my entrance.

"I'll go in nice and easy, baby. At first. Should be easier for you since you've got Xander's seed all up inside you."

Xander growled against my breast. The soft rasp of his beard against my very sensitive skin there only heightened the sensations.

Placing a hand on my shoulder, Tyler held me exactly where he wanted me as he slowly slid up and in. My body didn't resist as it had with Xander, the passage this time easy, just as he said. It could have been Xander's seed that eased the way or the knowledge that I could indeed handle big cocks. I didn't tense, just let him use my body. I didn't have much choice; his strong grip on my shoulder allowed me no movement and Xander had a tight hold on the tip of my breast with his teeth.

I could shift my hips as he moved in and out, but a surprising strike of his palm on my upturned bottom had me crying out and Xander letting me go.

"Stay still. Take what I give you." Tyler's voice held the command I'd come to recognize in Xander and it did things to me. Xander latched onto one nipple with his mouth once again and sucked. Hard. It wasn't as sharply painful as Tyler's tugging fingers, but the hot, wet tug sent spasms directly to my womb. He didn't linger on one nipple, but moved between the two as Tyler fucked me.

"God, I love hearing the wet suck of your pussy, the way my cock fucks and fills you. Xander's seed has made you so slippery." Tyler's voice only built my pleasure. I loved knowing I was satisfying both of them.

"It's time to come again, sweetheart," Xander said, his breath fanning over one damp nipple. "You're going to come because I tell you. You're going to come because I'm going to take that tight little tip in my mouth and nip it. Hard."

"Fuck, Xander, she just squeezed the hell out of my cock," Tyler said, his voice rough. He kissed the nape of my neck and nipped that tender skin.

I cried out and tossed my head back. My fingers and toes tingled, even the tips of my ears. It was as if every bit of pleasure coalesced between my legs; that my pussy had awakened for the first time. These two had wrung pleasure from me that I never knew was even possible. It made my skin damp with sweat, my breath catch in my throat, my heart race.

I couldn't hold back any longer. The feel of Tyler's cock hitting those newly discovered places inside of me and Xander's carnal words had me so close to the edge.

When Xander took my nipple into his mouth and licked it gently, I clenched down as Tyler thrust even harder. It was the anticipation that had me right... there.

When Xander's teeth sank into the tender tip, the pain radiated out from that tiny spot and spread throughout my body. Hotter and hotter I became until I burst, fire engulfing me. It was Tyler's cock though, that kept the feelings going, that made me cry out, gasp his name, wince as the pain at my breast morphed into the most decadent pleasure.

Tyler pulled me back onto his cock, seated himself into me fully as he groaned. I felt his release fill me as Xander's had, hot and pulsing. I felt claimed, completely and utterly taken. There was no question they'd made me theirs this first time.

I was lost under their spell. If they were going to

coax me into thinking that they were the men for me, they didn't need to do anything else. What just happened hadn't been lightning. It had been so, so much more, and I wanted it again.

And again.

9

XANDER

Tyler pulled out of Emily's pussy. I saw the regret on his face at doing so. I knew the feeling. I wanted to keep my cock deep inside of her forever. The hot feel of her, the way her inner muscles clenched and squeezed, the way she reacted as I moved inside her, were enough to make me want to never leave. But when Emily slumped down onto my lap as she recovered from her two orgasms, I relished the soft feel of her in my arms. She was so small, yet had the lushest curves. Feeling her silky skin, seeing the thin spider web of veins beneath the surface, even the sweet taste of her made me very possessive.

While in jail, I'd never imagined I'd have a woman to

call mine. I'd never thought I'd know the feelings that were brought about by a sweaty bout of fucking. Knowing my seed was deep inside her to make a child. Sharing her with my friend made it even better. To know that he would be just as protective, just as possessive of her as I was. Our combined seed mingled inside her, coated her and marked her. If we made a baby, hell, not if, but when, for we'd take her until she was ripe with child, it didn't matter who the father was. It would be ours as much as Emily was.

I didn't want anyone else to see her as we did, not like this, all sweaty and sticky with our seed, breathless and limp with satisfaction. Not her pale flesh, not the desire in her eyes, the surprise there at how we'd made her feel, the look of her as she came. I wanted to punch her dead husband for having her first. She was ours. If she doubted that, we'd just fuck her until she agreed.

"We're not done with you yet, sweetheart," I murmured.

She rubbed her face against my shirt.

"Why am I the only one naked?" she wondered.

I glanced up at Tyler, who was tucking his cock back in his pants. I'd only lowered mine enough to free my cock.

"Get used to it," he said. "You're going to be naked quite a bit from now on."

"Back up on your knees," I said.

She looked up at me and frowned. "Again?"

I chuckled at her expression, a mixture of surprise and arousal. My cock was quickly returning to readiness at the possibility. Instead, I grabbed the plug and held it up. Her eyes widened.

"Time for your ass training."

"Training?" she repeated, eyeing the plug with wariness and trepidation.

Tyler took it from me and helped Emily back up into position. Perhaps it was her relaxed and sated state that had her so pliable. It was something to remember if she was not eager for her ass to be stretched. Having her come a time or two first might make her more amenable.

From my vantage point, I could see between her thighs—shiny and sticky with our seed—that Tyler slowly pushed the plug up into her pussy. The wet sound of of it filling her was loud.

"Feel that? It's not as big as our cocks," Tyler said as he worked it slowly in and out, then left it inside of her. Using his right hand, he slid his fingers over her slick folds, then touched her ass.

I knew the moment he did it when her eyes widened in surprise. "Tyler!"

"Stay still. We'll hold you this time, but you *will*

present yourself for your training."

She shook her head. "No, I don't want to. It's going to hurt. I saw how Cross had his fingers inside of Olivia. I don't want that."

"Was she being hurt?" I asked.

She winced and groaned as Tyler continued to play. She shifted away.

"Stop moving." Tyler's words didn't keep her from trying to get away from his probing fingers.

I put my hands on her shoulders, held her still. "Reach back, Emily, grab your ass and spread yourself open for Tyler."

Her eyes widened. "What? I can't do that."

"You can and you will."

Tyler spanked her bottom.

"Tyler!" she cried, her legs tightening about my hips. "I don't want that plug."

"You want your husbands to claim you, don't you? This is so we don't hurt you. Like we said, Xander's going to fill your ass for the first time with his cock while I fuck your pussy. Together. But not until you're ready, until your ass is properly stretched."

"But—"

"Do you want him to spank you more?" I asked.

"No!"

"Then spread yourself open for him."

"I don't like this."

I had to get her mind to agree with her body, so I swiped my fingers through her wetness. Our seed. "This shows you like it. Remember, sweetheart." With my other hand, I reached up and stroked her hair back from her face. It had fallen loose from the pins as we'd fucked her. "We might not give you what you want. We'll give you what you need."

"I don't need to have that thing in me," she countered. I saw the heat in her eyes and this time it was in anger. My cock twitched at seeing her so riled.

"Two choices, baby," Tyler leaned down, kissed the nape of her neck, then murmured in her ear. "Reach back and hold yourself open for me or get spanked before you do it."

Her eyes narrowed as she stared at me. Slowly, she reached back and did as we said. I could see her hands holding herself open, but it was the pleased expression on Tyler's face as he moved back and looked at her that I knew she'd done as we said.

"Good girl," he said.

Tyler didn't delay. Slowly and carefully, he worked her with his finger, using the seed that coated her pussy as lubricant.

"What a pretty pink hole, baby. Are we the first to touch you here?"

She nodded as she held her breath, her breasts thrust out.

"She's tight. I'm in."

When her mouth fell open and she began to pant, I knew he was finger fucking her ass. Her dark eyes met mine and held. I watched the play of emotions I could see there. Anger, surprise, discomfort and finally, yes… arousal.

Tyler slipped the plug from her pussy. "This plug is nice and coated, baby. It's going to slide right in. Just like Xander's cock. Relax, take a deep breath and let it out. Good."

Her eyes widened and she groaned, long and low. While she didn't want to have her ass breached, she kept her hands in position.

I began to whisper to her. *Such a good girl. You're going to like having your ass fucked. We're going to take you together, one of us in your ass, the other in your pussy. We're going to get you between us and never let you go. That's it. Take more. Let the plug stretch you wide for our cocks. Ah, your nipples are all hard again. You like this, don't you?*

Tyler stepped back and I knew the plug was in.

"You can let go now, sweetheart," I said, but I didn't release the grip on her shoulders. She might have adjusted to having a plug deep in her ass, but I didn't want her to sit on my lap and bump it. Not yet, at least.

Her hands dropped to her sides and she looked away. A blush crept from her cheeks, down her neck and over her upturned breasts.

"Tyler, Emily came when we fucked her—without touching her clit."

I looked down her body and saw that little pink pearl jutting out from its protective hood.

Tyler scooped her up into his arms with a surprised gasp from Emily, then lowered to his knees before me. He turned her so her back rested against his chest with her ass on my lap. I parted her legs, placing her calves onto the cushioned armrest on either side of me. The way she was leaning back, her pussy and the plug that filled her ass were visible.

Her head rested against Tyler's shoulder and his hands cupped her breasts.

"You've been such a good girl, baby, that you get to just lie there and let us do the work now," Tyler said.

I touched the plug, liking the sight of the small handle snug against her stretched back entrance. Her pussy was slick and coated, her folds swollen and a bright cherry red. They were slightly parted and I could see her opening and the seed that slipped from it. Her clit was just as swollen and slick, eager for attention. Circling it with just the tip of my finger, I was careful with it. Exposed as it was, I knew it would be very sensitive.

"The way you came without having your clit stimulated while we fucked you shows how responsive you are to us. Our cocks can make you come. We're pleased."

"Fuck, yeah," Tyler added.

Her hips began to move as I discovered that her clit was more sensitive on the left side. Her eyes fell closed when she gave over. I loved to see her do that, to have her muscles relax, to have all the tension seep from her body as she gave herself to us.

"So beautiful."

It was Tyler's turn to whisper to her as I played, bringing her to orgasm easily. Once, twice and then again.

She was thrashing in my lap, her body slick with sweat, her nipples plump and red. They no longer tightened when she came, her body just overwrought with pleasure.

"I can't... it's too much. Please, the pleasure... it *hurts*," she cried.

A tear slipped from her closed eye.

"One more, sweetheart, because it pleases us. Your body is ours to pleasure." I flicked the very tip of her clit and she sighed, the slight tremor of her body the only indication she came. She went limp in Tyler's arms.

"Good girl," he whispered, lifting her up and carrying her up to bed. I stood, my cock hard again, and followed. If fucking your bride into sleep was indication that she was well satisfied, then we'd been successful in claiming her. Her body responded to us, knew us and would now be owned by us.

10

Emily

I awoke very warm. So warm I tried to push the covers down, but I realized it wasn't heavy blankets that had me overheated. It was two men. Xander and Tyler. I'd married them. I'd fucked them. I'd held open my bottom so Tyler could put a wooden object, much too large for such a place, deep inside me. I clenched down and felt it still inside.

The last I remember was being sprawled across Xander's lap. Tyler had supported me as I was brought to climax again and again. I'd had no idea that pleasure could become unbearable. It had been too much. *They* had been too much.

Even now, they surrounded me. Filled me.

"Morning, baby." I lifted my head and met Tyler's eyes. His hand stroked over my hip. "Sleep well?"

I offered a slight nod and felt Xander shift behind me. My head was on Tyler's shoulder and Xander was pressed up against my back like we were two spoons in a drawer.

"We wore you out last night," Xander said, his voice rough and deep with sleep.

The bedroom was lit with the soft pink of early morning. Through the open windows I heard the chirping of birds.

Yes, they'd worn me out and I flushed, remembering all that they'd done.

"Are you sore?" Tyler asked as Xander slipped from the bed. My back was cool from his absence.

I took stock of my body. I had that ridiculous plug in my bottom, which while wasn't sore, was odd. It wasn't even uncomfortable any longer. Perhaps my body had adjusted to it or it was simply that I'd been asleep and hadn't known it was there.

My pussy was a little sore, tender even. They hadn't taken me gently with their big cocks.

"Not much," I replied.

Tyler kissed my forehead before he climbed from the bed. He was naked.

Their Reluctant Bride

My eyes widened as I stared. While I might have been fucked by both of them, they'd remained clothed while doing so, only baring the most essential of areas. Now, I couldn't look away for I'd never seen a man so well formed. His broad chest tapered into a narrow waist, lean hips and long legs. Muscles defined every inch of him. As he grinned at me, I watched as his cock hardened, elongating and thickening, curving upward toward his navel from a thatch of light hair.

He went to a dresser and pulled out some clean clothes and started to put them on, the sinewy muscles of his back shifting with the movement.

While he did so, I turned my head. Sure enough, Xander was naked, too, on the other side of the room. Where Tyler had a bare chest, Xander's had a smattering of dark hair that tapered into a thin line that went directly to the base of his cock. He was also aroused. *Very* aroused.

"I... I did that to you?" I pointed at both of them.

"I like seeing those pretty breasts," Tyler said, tucking his cock into the front of his pants.

"He does like breasts, sweetheart. They're going to get plenty of attention from him. Me, I like seeing that plug part those ass cheeks."

I realized by Xander's words that I was bare to them. I was on my side and only my lower legs were covered.

As I reached to tug the covers over me, Tyler shook his head. "Never cover your body in front of your men."

I dropped my hand to the bed.

"We'd fuck you right now, but we need to meet the others for breakfast. Tell them we're leaving today."

I pushed myself upright. Tyler's eyes dropped to my chest. "Leaving?"

"We only came to Bridgewater to visit Olivia for a spell. Now that we have you, it's time to go home, to our own ranch and settle in. This isn't our house or our land."

I'd forgotten that. This was a good thing, leaving the area, especially before Saturday when Ralph expected me to just show up at the saloon, ready to lie on my back and part my legs for money. Perhaps Ralph wouldn't even know where I went and would forget about me and what I owed him. If he couldn't find me then my secret would remain safe.

This alone had me eager to rise. Tyler grabbed my shift off the back of the chair and tossed it onto the bed before me. He hadn't spent the time to button his shirt.

"Put on your shift and come downstairs. I'll heat some water on the stove for you to clean up." He ran a knuckle down my cheek, then left.

Xander finished dressing, then knelt on the bed, cupped his palm around the back of my neck and pulled

Their Reluctant Bride

me in for a kiss. A sweet one. A slow one. When his tongue dipped into my mouth, I gasped. He took that opportunity to plunder and I sank into it. I'd never been kissed with a man who had a beard. Well, I'd only been kissed by Frank before now, and in comparison, it was as if I'd been kissing a fish.

The beard was soft and it tickled, but it was forgotten as his tongue tangled with mine.

When he finally lifted his head, we were both breathing hard. "That was our first kiss," I said, touching my fingers to my lips. They tingled and felt swollen.

Xander's eyes darkened as he grinned. "On your mouth," he added. "I kissed your sweet pussy quite a bit yesterday."

I flushed at the reminder.

He pushed off the bed. "Get dressed and come down."

"Xander," I called. He turned in the doorway. I couldn't meet his eyes as I asked, "Um... what about the, um... what about the thing in my bottom?"

He grinned, the wicked man. "The plug? We'll take it out downstairs."

Downstairs? He expected me to walk downstairs with it in? I carefully moved to stand at the side of the bed and slip the shift over my head. I could feel the plug in me, filling me. Stretching me. As I moved across the room and down the hall, it moved too, nudging and bumping places deep inside me. While I knew it was firmly seated, I clenched down on it.

As I carefully walked into the kitchen, the men turned, smiled at me. Their gazes raked down my body, barely hidden beneath my shift. Tyler held out his hand. "Let's get that plug out of you."

I walked over to him gladly. I did not expect to be lifted up onto the table and pushed onto my back, however. "Tyler!" I cried. "What are you doing?"

He pushed my knees apart and then tugged at the end of the plug. I clenched down on the object even though I knew I had to relax to have it removed.

"Breathe, baby."

Tyler slowly pulled on it and I groaned as it widened, stretching me open, then hissed as it slid free. Tyler's finger pressed against my opening and slipped the tip of it into me.

"It worked well," Tyler commented. Xander moved to glance over his shoulder. "She's stretched nicely. I can slip my finger in, no problem."

That *was* a problem. I didn't want these two thinking that hole was an option, at least for a long while until I adjusted to the idea, to the feel of the plugs. They could fill my pussy all they wanted. In fact, I wished they'd pull out their big cocks and take me on the table.

"Tyler," I whined, embarrassed.

Tyler slipped his finger free and Xander handed him a damp cloth. He wiped me intimately, the warm water cleaning the dried seed from my skin. Just the feel of the cloth against my folds and over my clit had me shift my hips.

"Eager, are we?" Tyler asked, that grin making him look so handsome. "Xander, hand me the razor and soap."

Xander handed him a shaving cup, a brush inside, and set a razor on the table beside me.

"Tyler's going to shave your pussy, sweetheart. Get you nice and bare and smooth."

I frowned and tried to come up onto my elbows. "Why?"

"Because it's going to be so much more sensitive when we put our mouths on you. Trust us, sweetheart, you're going to love it." Xander's words didn't alleviate my confusion, but I didn't have time to argue. Tyler applied thick soap to the hair between my thighs, the bristles of the soft brush tickling my skin.

"Don't move. I don't want to nick this pretty pink flesh," Tyler said, holding the straight razor up for me to see just before he pulled my skin taut and shaved a small area bald. Again and again he did it, wiping the razor clean as he went.

When done, he stepped away and left Xander to look his fill, to stroke a finger over the bare skin. It was smooth, soft and just as sensitive as he'd said. Swiping his finger through the folds, he brought it to his mouth and licked it clean.

"Like honey, sweetheart."

I was wet and watching him suck my juices from his finger only made me wetter. He was so carnal, so virile I wanted him to take me again.

"Let's get you dressed before we fuck you here on the table and make you all dirty again." He held out his hand and helped me up and off the table.

"I will need to get my clothes from home," I said, remembering that I had nothing but the one dress.

"Home is with us now, baby," Tyler commented. "We'll stop and collect your things on the way."

Tyler tossed Xander my dress and he helped me into it, did the buttons for me.

"I need my corset," I said, when I realized I was only wearing my slip with my dress.

Xander finished up the remainder of the buttons, then cupped my breasts through the material. "Not today. We want easy access. It's a long ride. We may want to stop and fuck you on the way. To take the edge off our needs until we get you home and in bed. Our bed."

The idea had my folds getting damp.

"I like breasts, baby." Tyler tugged me to him and he wrapped his arm about my waist, holding me tight. I was being manhandled, bandied about between the two of them like a toy. Perhaps I was to their baser needs. I should have felt embarrassed about this as I did when they played with my ass, but I didn't. It felt... good. I hadn't had the attentions—good attentions—of a man before. Now I was the center of two men's attentions. They wanted me. There was no doubt. The difference between these two and Frank was that they weren't just taking. They were giving in return. In fact, I'd had many more orgasms than them. Combined.

"I like nipples. I like seeing *your* nipples all tight and hard." Tyler pushed me back and took his own turn cupping them. He could feel that my nipples had indeed tightened at their words. He growled. "You're bewitching." He swatted my bottom gently.

"Breakfast," Xander said, his voice almost a cranky growl. It seemed none of us wanted to join the others for the meal, instead eager for each other.

Tyler was wrong though. I wasn't the one who'd done the bewitching.

11

Tyler

"We weren't expecting you," Mason said, opening the door wide for us to enter. We'd walked the distance to his house—with Brody and their wife, Laurel—where the group congregated for the meals. As Kane, Ian and Emma had the biggest kitchen, it was usually served at their house—the house we'd been staying in—but had relocated for the duration.

Emily stood between us, Xander's hand at the small of her back. I liked having her in the middle, knowing she belonged to us and was ours to protect. What I didn't like was seeing the outline of her hard nipples through her dress. My cock hardened, which made walking uncomfortable. Perhaps skipping her corset wasn't such a good idea.

"We will eat and then be on our way," I told him. "It's time to return to our own ranch."

"Yes," Brody added as he came into the entry from the dining room. Laurel followed. "Kane and Ian's house is not where you should settle with your bride."

Xander nudged Emily toward the other woman and they walked off toward the kitchen together. While she was closest to Olivia, all of the women at Bridgewater were her friends. I was glad to see her comfortable here. She would eventually adjust to having two husbands, but it felt good knowing that Bridgewater would be a sanctuary for her, where there were others who understood her need to submit to two men, perhaps even when she might not.

"The food is on the table," Brody said, then went back into the dining room. The scent of fried potatoes and bacon filled the air.

We followed and the ladies joined us from the kitchen, Emily carrying a platter of sliced ham. We saved her a seat between us and I held out a chair for her. She paused and looked at Olivia and her men, who were already seated at the table. Color bloomed in her cheeks and she looked away. I'd forgotten about what she'd witnessed the day before.

Olivia stood and came around the table, took Emily's hand in hers.

"Don't be embarrassed. Please," she practically begged. "We are fast friends and I'd hate for anything to come between us." Olivia looked over her shoulder. "Especially my three very eager, very dominant husbands."

Emily glanced at her friend out of the corner of her eye. After biting her lip, she said, "I thought they were hurting you."

Olivia shook her head. "Hurt? No. I wasn't happy, at least there for a short time when they worked that thing into me." She'd leaned forward and grumbled the last, but I could still hear.

"She is a fierce friend," Simon said. Emily and Olivia both turned toward the man. "I thought she was going to shoot us."

I hadn't heard the part about a gun. I saw Xander sit up straighter at the reference.

Simon held up his hands as if we were holding a gun to him now. "She took the rifle off the wall. Came barging and would have shot anyone who hurt Olivia."

"Yes," Rhys added. "We are lucky our wife has such a friend."

Cross nodded his agreement.

I wasn't too keen on hearing my wife had been

waving a rifle around, but if Cross, Simon and Rhys were not bothered by the incident, then all I could do was to remember to teach Emily how to shoot.

Emily blushed again, this time for a completely different reason. I reached out and took Emily's hand, tugged her backward so I could wrap an arm about her waist. "Better now?" I asked.

She glanced at Olivia's men, who only had looks of respect on their faces.

She nodded and everyone returned to the meal. It was impressive how accepting she was. It could also have been the fact that we'd worked a plug into her ass just as Olivia's men had done to her. She could understand now. She might not have liked it in the moment, but she certainly screamed her pleasure when we'd brought her to orgasm with it filling her.

"You didn't wear the men out, Emily," Simon said as he cut a slice of ham.

I paused in my chewing. I expected a ribald comment or two since we had appeared directly after our wedding night and was glad it was directed at me and Xander. Simon obviously knew she'd had enough embarrassment for some time.

She scooped some potatoes onto her plate, then glanced up. "Oh?"

Cross passed me a pitcher of water.

"You are an *experienced* bride," Simon added. "I expected both men's cocks would be too sore for them to walk far." Laughter ensued and I couldn't help but shake my head. If we'd been at home, his statement would have been fairly accurate. Once there, I had no intention of letting her out of the bedroom for several days. As for now, Simon could clearly see that Emily was a well satisfied bride and I knew I couldn't help the content smile on my own face. By the way Xander looked, he might not even be surly for a time yet.

"I was gentle with them," Emily replied. "As they said, we have a long ride ahead today."

I couldn't help but grin as I leaned back and placed my arm over the tall back of Emily's chair. My fingers stroked her shoulder. I liked seeing her smile, seeing her finally at ease.

Simon laughed and pointed his fork at my bride. "Ah, Emily. I'm glad to see you have some spirit. You're going to need it with these two."

The meal was interrupted by heavy footfall on the front porch and everyone turned when Quinn, one of the ranch's foremen, held a man by his collar and pushed him into the room. The man stumbled, but Quinn jerked him upright.

"Found this man skulking about," Quinn said, not loosening his hold.

"I wasn't *skulking*," he replied, and tried to tug himself free, without any luck. Quinn held him fast and seemed more than eager to tear him limb from limb.

I recognized him from the picnic. He'd been the man who had made Emily unhappy, the man who we'd run off. What the hell was he doing here?

"Who are you and what are you doing on Bridgewater land?" Simon asked, standing to his very tall height. He made Xander and me seem like growing adolescents.

Out of the corner of my eye, I saw Emily stiffen, her back ramrod straight. Her fork clattered onto her plate. Based on the fact that neither Simon nor Quinn knew the man and Emily was not eager to see him—again—it was clear he was here because of her.

Xander must have come to the same conclusion because he stood when I did, our chairs scraping against the wood floor. I placed a hand on Emily's small shoulder. I felt her shudder beneath my palm and was glad she was sheltered between us. If this man meant to harm her, he'd have to get past both of us, and all of the Bridgewater men in the room.

"Explain yourself," Xander said, tossing his napkin onto the table.

The man turned his gaze to Emily and pointed a dirty, stubby finger. "She owes me money."

I heard Emily gasp. How the hell did she get involved with this bastard? The answer didn't matter at the moment. I just wanted him gone.

"How much?" I asked.

His eyes widened, then narrowed with obvious avarice. "Fifty dollars."

Xander reached into his pocket and pulled out his billfold. Rounding the table, he counted out the money before handing it to the man. Xander didn't step back, but loomed over him with his hands on his hips. With Quinn at his back, the man didn't dare make trouble and he knew it.

"Consider yourself paid," Xander said, his voice cold. "Now get the hell out of here." He pointed toward the front door.

Quinn tugged on his shoulder, pulling him back toward the entry. "I'll see that he gets off Bridgewater land."

"Much obliged," Xander said, with a nod of his head.

When the men's steps could no longer be heard, Xander returned to his chair. "Sorry, Brody, Mason," he nodded at both men. "I know this is your house and you should have been the ones to toss him out."

Brody held up his hand. "You were protecting your woman." He said nothing more as he glanced to Laurel

Their Reluctant Bride

in a way that said he'd have killed the man if he had been here for her.

"If you'll excuse us, we have some things to discuss with our bride," I said to the room at large. I was angry. Furious. Fucking frustrated.

I reached down and clasped Emily's elbow with a gentleness that belied my mood, helping her to her feet, then guiding her out of the dining room. While she wasn't resisting, she wasn't eager either. Xander went down a long hall and stuck his head in one door, then another. We followed into an office and he closed the door behind us. Only the ticking of a clock on the mantel of an unlit fireplace made noise. That and Emily's quick breaths.

"Who is he?" I asked, when we both turned to face her.

She looked down at the floor, her shoulders slumped. Her recently flushed cheeks were now pale.

"His name is Ralph." The sound of her voice was nothing like a few moments earlier when she was joking with Simon.

"How do you know him?" Xander asked.

She spun around, her eyes wild as she pointed at herself. "Me? I don't. Frank knew him."

Shit. Her gambler husband owed the man money

and he'd been pestering Emily for it. "Is that why he was talking with you at the picnic?"

She looked out the window, but nodded. Her hands played in the folds of her dress.

"Is that why you married us? So we'd pay your debt?" Xander's words were harsh. It was an angle I hadn't considered.

Shit. He thought she'd been using us. Perhaps she had. Without even knowing her answer, I could see why she'd done it, why a woman would choose us to protect her from the likes of that bastard. Xander, though, had a dark soul. He wasn't trusting like I was. He'd trusted in the past and paid a terrible price.

"We're rich. You knew that," he continued.

She slowly lifted her head and met Xander's hard stare. Her entire face held no expression, her eyes almost dead.

"You could have just asked." Xander's lips thinned as he ran a hand over his beard. "Any one of the Bridgewater men would have given him the money. You didn't have to marry us."

Tears streamed down her cheeks, but that was the only indication of her feelings.

"He's gone, but you're stuck with us, sweetheart."

When he said the endearment, there wasn't any warmth to it.

"You want me to tell you I married you for love?" she asked, her voice low. "You don't love me. You desire me. You proved that last night. But, love?" She shook her head. "No. You wanted me for your own reasons."

She was right. While I felt a connection with her, a bond that was strong enough to want me to marry her, I didn't love her. At least not yet. I barely knew her. The way she was standing up to Xander, the way she must have had to deal with Ralph, not to mention her husband before he died, had me admiring her. She didn't deserve an asshole for a husband. She didn't deserve to be left as a penniless widow. She didn't deserve to be hounded by a man who wanted money. Hell, maybe she didn't even deserve us.

"You got what you want." Xander placed his hands on his hips. "Now, it's time for you to give us what we want."

His intent was clear.

Emily didn't break his gaze as she swallowed, then calmly turned and leaned over the desk. Reaching back with an indifference born of experience, she lifted up her dress so that it bunched at her waist. Her gorgeous ass was round and curved over the edge.

"Jesus," I whispered, pissed that she'd done it with such easy acceptance. I stared hard at Xander, wanted to punch him in the face. "She bent over the desk thinking you want to fuck her as payment."

Xander stepped up to her, ran a hand over one pale globe and she flinched. "You think we want a whore?" He spanked her and she gasped. "We didn't marry you to be our whore. That's not what I want from you now."

She looked over her shoulder, confusion marring her smooth brow. "Then what *do* you want from me?"

"Honesty. We gave the man money and you'll give us the truth."

Damn straight.

"I told you the truth!" She tried to rise, but Xander pressed a hand at the small of her back and held her down. A pink handprint was forming on her pale skin.

"I went to jail for six months because of a lying woman," he admitted.

I moved to stand at the side of the desk so I could watch her face, saw her stunned expression at his admission. It was clear the Bridgewater ladies hadn't told her.

"Ralph came to you for money?" I asked. She looked up at me with her dark, sad eyes. "When?"

"The day I buried Frank. Said Frank owed him money because he'd lost playing cards."

"Did you give him any?" Xander asked.

"What money?" she asked, her tone dry. "The bank's

Their Reluctant Bride

taking the ranch, the furniture. Everything. I even offered for him to take whatever he wanted in payment before the bank took it away. He didn't want it. He wants *me*. Everyone in town knows my husband was a drunk and a gambler."

I'd heard it from various sources, but didn't realize the extent of her husband's troubles. Most men went to the saloon now and again and played a game of cards. But to lose a successful ranch and still owe money, that was something else entirely. And Emily had been mixed up in it all. Trapped, even.

"Then why did you target us?" Xander asked. It wasn't how I'd have phrased the question, but it made her respond.

She pursed her lips and narrowed her eyes. "I didn't *target* you two, you big brute. *You* asked *me*."

"You were desperate though. Desperate enough to say yes," Xander said, pushing her.

"That's right. I was desperate enough to say yes," she repeated, her words dripping with bitterness. "I assumed if he ever came around that you'd protect me. You're both much bigger than he is and that when he saw you both, he'd just give up the money owed him. Besides, your ranch isn't near here. I'd hoped he wouldn't know where I'd gone." When neither of us said anything, she continued. "What was I to do? He was going to make me work on my back as repayment."

Xander pushed down the back of her dress and stepped back as if he'd been burned. Spinning on his heel, he rubbed a hand over his beard and swore. Now he saw the error of his ways. His line of questioning made her think we were just like Ralph, that we just wanted her body.

"He was going to make you whore for him?" I asked. Anger bubbled to the surface and I clenched my fists. It was a good thing Quinn had dragged the man away, that enough time had passed where I couldn't go after them.

She came up slowly, clearly worried we'd push her back over the desk. "Saturday. I was supposed to go to him on Saturday."

"Fuck!" Xander shouted.

Emily flinched. I took her arm and helped her to stand. I pulled her into my arms, held her tightly, one hand at the nape of her neck, the other about her waist. I didn't care if she wanted me to hold her; I wanted to feel her in my arms.

"I'm sorry, baby," I murmured, kissing the top of her head. "You've been through so much. Sounds like your husband was quite the asshole."

She laughed, although it was full of sorrow.

Over her head, I glanced at Xander, who was

running his hands through his hair, tugging on it. His gaze was on Emily, looking at her as if he had no idea what to do with her. She was a puzzle, a mystery to him. Living on a sprawling ranch, he'd kept himself at a distance from people easily enough. As his friend, I understood him, his "think the worst of people" mentality. He also knew I wouldn't stand for any shit. But he was now responsible for Emily, which meant he would have to think and act differently from now on. The question was, would his past drive a wedge between the three of us? Could he be the man she needed?

12

Xander

Shit. *Shit.* What the fuck had I done? When that man had said he wanted money out of Emily, I hadn't thought about how he might be using her, but how *she* had been using *us*. I'd been stupid, fucking stupid. She'd even leaned over the desk and lifted her dress up, expecting us to get payment from her pussy. I was no better than Ralph.

"Did Frank hit you?" I asked. I tried to calm my racing heart, to take deep breaths and try not to scare her any more than I already had. People would walk a wide path around me on good days; between the two of us, Tyler had the sunny disposition. Emily needed her men to cherish her, not scare the hell out her.

Tyler held her tightly as if he could absorb all her pain—pain that I'd caused. I had to know the shadows of her heart, to know how she'd been hurt in the past so I didn't repeat it.

"A few times." Her voice was muffled by Tyler's shirt. He loosened his grip—slightly. "He was always drunk and I'd hidden the house money."

The idea of anyone laying a hand to her, especially her *husband*, the person who should have been taking care of her, had me wanting to hit something. Someone. But that wasn't what she needed right now.

She'd given the truth and she deserved it from me in return. I had to fix this, and the only way I could think of was to let her know about the man she married. She just caught a decent glimpse of him. I wasn't soft. I wasn't kind. Good thing she was legally married to Tyler. If need be, I could just ride off and leave them. She'd be safe and well cared for with him. My breakfast settled heavily in my stomach at the idea of never seeing her smile or see the way she came all over my cock again, knowing I'd given her the pleasure she deserved.

"I was convicted of a crime I didn't commit."

Emily twisted out of Tyler's hold and he dropped his hands, only long enough to pull her back into him, his arm banded about her waist. He was keeping her close and I didn't blame him.

"I was in Laramie and I spent the evening at the saloon. I'd had too much whiskey and I woke up the next day in a jail cell. The sheriff told me I'd almost beaten a woman to death. There were two witnesses."

As I spoke, my gut churned, remembering how I'd felt at the time. Hungover, definitely. Confused. I'd been railroaded and I hadn't even known how.

"I couldn't remember a thing. It was possible I'd actually done it."

"Bullshit," Tyler said.

I glanced up at my friend and knew he'd been as helpless as I in the situation.

"Weren't you there with him?" Emily asked, looking over her shoulder at Tyler.

I shook my head, answering for him. "I went for business alone. A cattle deal. Instead, I ended up before the circuit judge and then six months in jail."

"Surely you didn't hit a woman. You wouldn't do that!" Her vehemence melted a hardened spot on my heart. Even after the accusations I'd made, she stood up for me.

"After what I've just done to you, you're so sure?"

"Yes," she replied simply.

Their Reluctant Bride

The corner of my mouth tipped up. "You like it when I take control, sweetheart?"

She nodded, then bit her lip.

"You like it when I push you up against a door and lick your pussy until you come?"

I saw heat flare in her eyes, her flush creep down her neck. "Yes."

"I can't be gentle, sweetheart, but I'll never hurt you."

"I know."

Just like that, my cock hardened, my body relaxed and settled into the mindset of a man who had a woman who needed to be controlled. Who liked it. Who came because of it. Who *needed* it.

I flicked my gaze to Tyler and he just gave me a small nod. Emily wasn't leaving me. She wanted me just the way I was.

"You've been such a good girl, I think you deserve a treat."

I grinned when I saw her mouth fall open and her nipples tighten beneath her dress.

13

*E*MILY

"Treat?" I asked.

Xander had made my emotions so topsy-turvy that my brain was muddled. When Ralph had been dragged inside I thought my heart had stopped. He was insane to come to the Bridgewater Ranch and push me for money. He could have been shot and buried where no one would ever find the body. Xander and Tyler had protected me, paid the man and gotten rid of him all within a matter of a few short minutes.

I'd wanted them to protect me from Ralph but hadn't expected them to pay him off. Panic was replaced by relief when I knew he wouldn't be coming after me anymore. I was free of him once and for all.

But then Xander had accused me of awful things. I'd even thought he had wanted repayment in the form of... of fucking. I'd assumed then that he was no better than Ralph or Frank. So I'd dutifully bent over the desk as I'd assumed he'd want to take me. The look on his face when I'd done so was a mixture of anger and horror.

Then, hearing about his past, the reason for his abrupt and hard demeanor had my heart aching for him. What he'd gone through must have been awful for him, a man so desperate for control. I understood now why he wanted it when we were together, when he'd told me the other day he wanted me to submit.

I wasn't submitting to him like I had with Frank, with nothing in return. I was giving myself to Xander and he took that as a gift and cherished it.

I'd said I didn't love them. I didn't, but after Xander's confession, I knew it would happen given time. But would they ever love me? Xander spoke of hating liars. I was one. I hadn't told them about killing Frank. Keeping that secret was like keeping a lie, for they would never know the kind of woman they married. *I* was the lie. While I hadn't tried to pin my crime on an innocent person, I'd definitely gotten away with it.

"A treat, sweetheart," Xander repeated. His voice,

while still commanding, had lost the hard edge. He was still full of intent, but it had shifted. "Not a candy or anything, although I'll find it very sweet."

I frowned, not sure what he meant.

"Hold up your skirt for me. More. More."

I lifted the fabric so the bottoms of my legs were exposed. First my ankles, then my calves, then higher and higher until I knew to what he spoke.

I felt Tyler at my back as his hands cupped my breasts. Only for a moment did he squeeze and fondle them, for he moved them to work the buttons down my dress so that my breasts were revealed to their gazes, so he could play with them without the dress in the way.

Xander dropped to his knees before me when I held the fabric up around my waist, just as it had been only the day before. Instead of the unforgiving hard door at my back, I had Tyler, all rippling muscle and hot skin. Xander pushed my thighs apart, kissed the soft skin there on one side, then the other. The rasp of his beard made my skin tingle, a sharp contrast to his soft lips. He glanced up at me, his dark eyes filled with arousal and a hint of pleading. "I won't be gentle in this, Emily, but I will pleasure you."

Through my instant haze of arousal, I saw the kiss for what it had been. Gentle. Xander didn't see it or even know he had it in him.

When his fingers slid inside of me as his mouth latched onto my clit, I knew he would pleasure me as he'd said. There was no question. In fact, he didn't tease, didn't start off slowly, but curled his fingers over a place inside of me that had my hips bucking and a gasp escaping my lips.

His tongue slid over my newly bare flesh and I had to admit it was much more sensitive. When he flicked against my clit as he sucked on it, working me up to the peak within seconds, I would never doubt them again.

When Tyler tugged on my nipples, then pinched them, I couldn't hold back. I was so easy to arouse. I came with a breathy scream.

"Xander, yes!"

I wilted against Tyler, my breathing ragged, limp like a rag doll. I realized that my fingers were tangled in Xander's dark hair and holding his face against my pussy.

Releasing my hold, he pulled back and glanced up at me from his intimate spot. His lips and beard gleamed with my arousal. Slowly, he slipped his fingers from me, then licked them clean.

"So sweet," he murmured before standing, then lacing a hand behind my neck. "Taste."

He lowered his head and kissed me, his tongue dipping into my mouth and I tasted Xander's personal flavor, but my own as well. I was sweet and musky and the combination was heady.

"I hope you're not hungry, for I want to get home as quickly as possible."

Tyler grunted in reply. "We would fuck you now, baby, but I doubt Brody and Mason want to give up their office for the rest of the day."

With awareness came embarrassment. "Oh, I'm sure they heard me. What are they going to think?"

I covered my face with my hands.

"They'll think you have two very skilled lovers."

I peeked between my fingers at them. They stood before me with open arousal and, when I glanced down at the front of their pants, very hard cocks. It was their grins, however, that had me pulling my hands back and laughing with them. It was amazing, the change in my mood after a husband-induced orgasm.

"Of course, I'm thrilled!" Tyler's mother exclaimed when I was introduced.

We'd ridden to Helena and made good time, arriving at Tyler's parents' house before the sun set. Xander said it was a good halfway point to the ranch and where we would spend the night.

Their Reluctant Bride

I knew the Bridgewater men were wealthy. I even knew Tyler and Xander had money—if it hadn't been Xander giving Ralph fifty dollars directly from his billfold, it was the information Olivia had shared about her cousin's ranch. But the mansion in which Tyler was raised was much more obvious. So far I'd counted three servants, all of whom Tyler knew by name.

I'd expected a stodgy older woman with a diamond-covered chip on her shoulder, but I was very wrong. Mrs. Tannenbaum was relaxed and delightful. She hugged the ever-stiff Xander and even coaxed a smile from him. Instead of eating a late meal in their formal dining room, we sat at a well-used table in the kitchen.

"I knew the two of you would find a bride together, but not this week." She was pleased and overwhelmed with the news. "I am sorry your fathers are not here to see you. They would have stalled their meeting in Billings had they known."

She ran a hand down her son's cheek, the love there quite clear. I felt a pang of jealousy for what they shared; I never knew my mother, as she died when I was a baby and I did not wish to remember my father.

"As you always said—"

"Lightning."

The one word had Tyler nodding.

Mrs. Tannenbaum turned toward me. "Tell me about yourself, Emily."

Her posture was ramrod straight and her hands were folded in her lap. She was a lady through and through.

I dabbed my lips with my napkin and took a sip of water. I cleared my throat, suddenly nervous. *I am a liar. A killer.* "Well, Mrs. Tannenbaum—"

"Belinda, please."

I gave a small nod. "All right. Belinda. I was recently widowed and found myself in a predicament." I didn't need to share more than that and I was relieved neither man chose to do so. I glanced at both of them. Tyler watched me with his usual calm demeanor—now I knew where it came from—and Xander was helping himself to a second serving of chicken and dumplings.

"It wasn't a good marriage," Belinda said. She didn't form it as a question, but as fact. She was very good at reading people, so I looked away. What else could she see?

"No. It wasn't a good marriage. He wasn't a good man." That truth was easy to tell. "Marrying Xander and Tyler, well, it might not have been lightning as you call it..." I swallowed again, worried I'd make everyone mad at me. Perhaps she'd see me as a gold digger even, or worse, what I really was. "However, I have found that both Xander and Tyler are... nice."

Their Reluctant Bride

Xander arched a brow and his forkful of dumpling stopped halfway to his mouth. "Nice? You think that about us?"

I shrugged, not wanting to admit to my new mother-in-law that I found her son and Xander very attractive and eager to have them fuck me as soon as we were in private.

"We will have to work on some other adjectives," Tyler added with a very heated look.

I felt my cheeks blush.

"A woman marries for completely different reasons than a man. Look at these two." Belinda waved her hand between the men. "They have money, looks, land, a successful business. They do not need to account to anyone. A woman, though, can't work, but if she did, it would be at a backbreaking task and for a piddly amount. She would be vulnerable to less honorable men and her virtue would be constantly in question."

While Xander started eating again, he listened carefully.

"As for you, a widow, I assume you had no protection once you were alone. Do you have family?"

I placed my napkin on the table beside my plate. "No, ma'am."

Tyler stood, retrieved the coffeepot from the stove and filled his mug.

"Marrying for protection is reason enough. A man must understand this and be *gentle*—" she looked blatantly at Xander, then at Tyler, "—and *patient*."

"Point taken, Mother," Tyler said, sitting back down, his long legs stretched out beneath the table.

She was so *kind*. How would she feel about me when she learned I was a killer? God, the guilt, the worry, it was getting worse and worse. My secret was a weapon for so many people. I didn't intend to hurt any of them, but the list of casualties was growing.

"You do not have any children?" She looked at me almost wistfully.

I looked down at my empty plate. I was a liar and possibly barren. I was a terrible wife. The guilt about both riddled me. "No."

"I could only have Tyler, but I had Olivia to raise as well after her parents died. I'm sure these two will get you with child soon enough."

My cheeks burned at her bold words.

"Mother!" Tyler shouted, rolling his eyes.

Xander made a sound in the back of his throat.

Belinda did not look mollified at all. "I want grandchildren."

She stood. Xander and Tyler did as well. "I will let you get to that task. You're newlyweds. You don't need your mother about, but I am glad you came here. You know the way to your rooms." She came around and gave me a generous hug, the swirl of soft perfume circling about. She kissed her son, then slid her hand down Xander's upper arm as she left the room.

"Don't be embarrassed," Tyler told me. "If it means getting grandchildren, hell, she'll lock us in the bedroom until our seed takes. One perk of a woman having two husbands like her is that she's well aware of their needs." He chuckled.

"You mean fucking," I replied, glancing between the two of them.

"Hell, yes," Xander added, running a hand over his beard.

Tyler took a step closer, cupped the back of my head. "As for grandchildren..."

"What if I can't have any? I... miscarried once and then no success after that." I worried my lip. What if I couldn't fulfill the most important role of a wife, for not only one man, but two?

Tyler kissed the top of my head. "I'm sorry to hear that, baby. That must have been very sad for you. Perhaps the problem with making babies wasn't with you, but Frank. As for making babies with us, well, we've fucked you enough to have it be a possibility."

"Just to be sure, we're going upstairs right now and

we're going to fill you up with our seed all night long." Xander didn't leave any room for confusion.

"Damn straight," Tyler added. Bending his knees, he tossed me over his shoulder and carried me up the back stairs. If I couldn't have a baby, it wasn't going to be for lack of trying.

"But..." I couldn't say anything more. I tried, but the air kept getting bumped and jostled from me.

14

Tyler

I dropped Emily onto the large bed. She bounced once and then settled. Her hair was falling from its pins, her eyes wide with surprise and her cheeks flushed. She looked wanton and decadent and I couldn't wait to get her clothes off so I could touch every part of her. To make her cry out her pleasure.

Fucking in the past had been all about the release, the ability to lose myself in the pleasure of it. With Emily, it was so much more than that. I wanted to please *her*. It was half the fun of it. Perhaps in about a decade or so we'd discover all the different ways to make her wet. In the meantime, we were going to have fun finding them.

"It's a good thing your ass isn't ready yet for our cocks, sweetheart. We want every drop of our seed in that sweet pussy of yours until we give you that baby you want," I commented as I began to undo the buttons of my shirt.

Xander lit the lantern beside the bed, bathing the room in a soft glow.

"You want children?" she asked, looking between us. Xander stood beside me so we were shoulder to shoulder above her.

"Hell, yes. A little girl who looks just like you," I said, watching as tears filled her eyes.

Xander flicked a look my way at her unexpected response. "I never thought it would be a possibility. The idea of your belly swelling with our child..." Xander groaned.

To my surprise, Emily rolled off the side of the bed and began pacing the room, crying in earnest.

I looked to Xander, who frowned.

I knew women to be moody sometimes, but this... this was something different. I did know we had to tread lightly. I'd seen my fathers trying to soothe my mother before. It took a gentle hand.

Their Reluctant Bride

"What's wrong?" I asked.

She shook her head and began to mumble as she cried. I couldn't understand her, but heard a few words. Liar. Trouble.

I caught her as she walked by us and pulled her into my arms, but she struggled away and leaned forward, covering her face with her hands.

What the hell did we do? Gentle persuasion wasn't working. Kindness wasn't working. Shit. I hated crying women. I ran my hand over the back of my neck. "Emily... shh."

"Stop," Xander said, his voice booming in the otherwise quiet room.

Emily sucked in a breath and she dropped her hands. She stopped crying. Xander had, perhaps, scared the tears from her, but it had worked. She stared at him, mouth open.

"Take off your clothes," Xander commanded.

I put a hand on his arm. "What if she's upset because she doesn't want to fuck?"

"That's not it," he replied. How he could be so sure, I had no idea. "Are you afraid to fuck us, sweetheart?"

She shook her head, her cheeks tearstained and pale.

"Take off your clothes," he repeated. "All of them."

Emily paused for the briefest of moments, but did as Xander said. No, commanded. She was submitting to him. The problem wasn't solved, but she was responding. Perhaps Xander was right. Perhaps even Emily was right. She liked rough and he liked to dominate.

Quickly enough, she was naked before us, her dress, shift, stockings and boots a small pile on the floor between us. Her nipples tightened before our eyes.

Xander lifted his chin. "Turn around and put your hands on the edge of the bed. Good. Now lean onto your forearms."

Emily settled into the position Xander expected, her head down, her ass up and out.

"This is how you want to talk with her?" I asked, worried she might start crying all over again. "Earlier, she was in this position over a desk and thought we wanted to fuck her."

"This isn't about fucking. Spread your legs. Wider." Obviously, he was ignoring my concerns for Emily. "Good girl." Xander's voice, while deep, had an almost soothing quality to it and I couldn't miss the way Emily sighed, her body relaxing.

He looked at me. "Yes, this is how we're going to talk with her. She likes it. I know because she's wet."

Their Reluctant Bride

Her bare pussy was exposed and I could see her folds gleam with her arousal, although Xander chose to swipe one blunt finger over them so even Emily was aware. She gasped, her hips twitched, but she remained in place.

"She knows we won't hurt her. Right, Emily?"

"You won't hurt me," she replied, the sound muffled by the blanket. She sniffed once, then again.

"We will spank you."

She stiffened then, but Xander placed his palm on her lower back.

"Have you been bad, Emily?"

Xander's hand moved lower, stroking over one pale globe.

She nodded.

Spank.

"You're going to give the problem to your men, sweetheart."

Spank.

"We need to listen to her, not spank her," I told him. He was pushing her too far.

Xander lifted his hand, then spanked a different spot on her ass. The skin instantly turned a pretty shade of pink. Emily cried out, but remained in place.

"She needs this. She needs to let it out." *Spank.* "She

won't share. Whatever it is, she's guilt-ridden over it." He tilted his chin again. "Can't you see? She needs me—us—to take over. She wants to tell us but doesn't know how. We will take her decision away. It's not her choice now, but ours."

Spank, spank.

The strikes weren't hard. She never once lifted up onto her toes or cried out in pain. Xander was careful, watching her reaction each time his palm struck.

"What did you do, Emily?" Xander asked after a time.

She was crying in earnest now, but she wasn't tense any longer. She'd long ago relaxed into each spank, allowing it. Taking it. Giving in.

"I did it!" she cried.

Spank.

I could see now that she responded to this unorthodox attention. How Xander somehow knew what she needed, I had no idea. Thank Christ he could read her when I couldn't.

"Did what, baby?" I asked. I matched Xander's deep tone.

"I killed him."

Xander's hand paused in mid-air and he looked to me, his eyebrows going up. Did she say *killed*? Catching himself, he pulled his hand back and

Their Reluctant Bride

spanked her. I could see now she needed no reaction on our part besides domination. If we faltered, so would she.

"Who?" he asked, his voice the same even tone.

"Frank," she cried as Xander spanked her again. Her crying came out in deep sobs now.

Xander didn't stop, but by the sound of his hand on her red ass alone, I could tell he'd lightened up a little. He peppered her flesh over and over until the entire lush surface glowed hotly.

She'd killed her husband. He hadn't died falling down the steps, drunk. What had he done to her to warrant her to do such a thing? There was no way in hell Emily would do something like that without being provoked. She wasn't a murderer. She'd gone to Olivia's rescue with a rifle, facing off against three big men. Simon, Cross and Rhys wouldn't have hurt her, but she'd taken that risk to protect her friend.

When her tears had subsided somewhat, Xander asked, "How?"

"I... I hit him with a frying pan."

Xander's hand fell to his side and for a moment, we just stared at her, bent over with her ass upturned.

A frying pan?

Xander scooped her up and sat on the bed, her head tucked beneath his chin. When she hissed as her ass came in contact with his thighs, Xander shifted her so she sat more comfortably.

I knelt down before her, stroked my hand over her cheek, my thumb wiping away the remainder of her tears. Seeing her like this was heart-wrenching.

"What did he do to you?"

"He was drunk." She hiccupped, then sniffed. "He wanted money that I'd hid from him. He needed to give it to Ralph, but I refused. It was the money for food, for the house." She took a deep breath, then continued. "He came after me as I knew he would. I used the only weapon I had at hand."

"You hit him with a frying pan?"

She nodded against Xander's chest. "He said he was going to... to whip me, then take his husband's rights."

Jesus. I glanced up at Xander. He'd just spanked her and I hadn't stopped him.

As if Xander could read my thoughts, he murmured, "Not the same thing."

I wasn't so sure about that.

"So you were in the kitchen and he came after you?"

She shook her head again. "I was upstairs in the bedroom. He woke me up. I'd taken the frying pan with me because he'd become angrier the more he gambled. I was afraid of him."

"Why didn't you tell us?" Xander asked.

Their Reluctant Bride

Emily pulled back, looked between us. With her blotchy face and messy hair, she looked so lost, vulnerable.

"I thought you wouldn't want me," she admitted. "Why would you want a murderer for a wife? But I had to find some way to save myself from Ralph's plan to have me work in the saloon. I would have told you when you learned about Ralph, but Xander had said he hated liars and that's what I am."

She sniffed again.

I frowned. "Did you kill him on purpose?"

Her eyes widened. "No!" she cried, then hopped up from Xander's lap. She began pacing once again and I doubted she even remembered she was naked. "He was going to hurt me." She spun to face us, her eyes wild. "He was, truly. You have to believe me. He'd hit me before and this time he was so mad."

"I believe you," Xander said plainly.

"I believe you, too. It was self-defense, plain and simple," I added.

"But I pushed him down the stairs, made it look like he fell."

Xander stood and walked over to her, pulled her back into his arms, his hand stroking up and down her spine. "That was smart. Most men, sheriffs, judges even, don't see the gray area in the law. What you did was wrong, but you saved yourself."

Xander knew from experience that some lawmen did not work for justice.

"We'd have killed him if we'd known how he'd hurt you. The Bridgewater men would have, too."

She looked surprised, hopeful even. "You don't hate me?" she asked, her voice querulous.

I stood, too. "Hate you?" I tugged her from Xander's arms, pulled her into mine. "We admire you. You're so strong. So brave. You shouldn't have had to carry that alone, baby."

"There should be no secrets between us," Xander said.

Emily reached out her arm and Xander grasped her hand. "Ralph. He knows. I don't know how, but he knows what I did. He threatened to tell you. To ruin us."

I ground my back teeth together. How I wished Quinn hadn't dragged him away. I'd have hit him with more than a frying pan.

She'd said "to ruin *us*." The sound of it soothed something inside me, the place where I worried that she wouldn't want us, that Xander was too rough, that I was too mild, that we weren't what she needed. But the use of the word "us" indicated that she considered us to be a family, a unit. She felt she was already ours.

Looking to Xander over Emily's head, I could read his thoughts. He'd caught that, too. But that wasn't all. There was Ralph and he could affect *us*. The bastard would be back. He wouldn't stop with just fifty dollars if he could have more. Bribery, extortion. It wasn't beneath the likes of him.

15

Emily

"Morning, sweetheart," Xander murmured from between my spread thighs.

I looked down my body at him, his eyes hooded perhaps from sleep, but more likely with arousal. Just the sight of him there, his hands on my inner thighs, was so decadent. Frank had never put his mouth on my pussy, ever. If Tyler liked my breasts, then Xander definitely liked to lick my pussy.

His finger was curled deep inside of me, pressing against that special spot, rubbing it so that my hips arched—directly into his mouth. How had I slept through him settling between my thighs? How had I

Their Reluctant Bride

been unaware of his blunt finger sliding into me? I could feel their slick seed still deep within. His beard rasped against my newly bare pussy and when he flicked my clit with his tongue, then sucked on it, I came.

My eyes fell closed and I cried out. He could work my body so easily; I was so responsive to him. I wilted against the bed, ready to fall back asleep.

As Xander kissed his way up my body, he murmured, "So sensitive after last night. I love the way your body responds."

Sitting back on his heels, he grabbed my hips and flipped me over onto my belly. I gasped at the surprise, but I was getting used to his more aggressive touch. Smoothing a hand over my bottom, he commented, "Not even red this morning. Is it sore?"

Coming up onto my elbows, I looked at him over my shoulder. I was too sated and sleepy to feel embarrassed. "Are you referring to the plug stretching me or the spanking last night?"

Xander had spanked me. I'd... I'd loved it. At first, it had surprised me, but his commands, his deep voice was like a rope keeping me tethered to safety. I'd been lost, overwhelmed, completely blanketed by guilt at what I'd done, what I'd subjected the men to. But Xander's commands had altered my focus. The first spank had been like a bucket of cold water, jolting me from my thoughts and forcing me to focus solely on him. The sting of his palm, the tingling heat of my skin.

I'd been able to think only of that instead, to give in to it. Xander hadn't stopped. I couldn't think, couldn't do anything but accept he had taken over. The truth had slipped from me easily then. Like my body, I'd handed the problem over to them. I'd thought they would hate me, but they hadn't. In fact, from the looks on their faces, they'd have killed Frank themselves, and not by accident.

He gave me a light, playful swat and grinned.

Tyler came into the room then with a tray, closing the door behind him. "Leaving me out?" he asked.

"After last night, you feel left out?" Xander asked.

They'd both taken me, one after the other, again and again. While they'd each been given time to recover, long enough for the other to fuck me, I'd had none. They'd given me orgasm after orgasm and even now, I could feel their seed seeping from me. To say they'd filled me was a gross understatement.

"We can't leave the room before noon," Tyler said. "My mother will think we aren't attentive enough toward our new bride otherwise."

Xander laughed softly and shook his head. It was clear to me he wasn't used to a mother any more than me.

"Emily was just speaking about the plug in her ass," Xander replied.

Tyler's brow went up as he placed the tray on a table beneath a large window. I could smell coffee and cinnamon rolls. My stomach rumbled and Xander offered another light swat to my bottom.

"Think your ass is ready for our cocks, baby?" Tyler asked as he came over to sit beside me on the bed. He reached down and took hold of the hard base that was keeping my cheeks parted. Tugging on it, I groaned, then clenched.

"I... I don't know," I replied as I took deep breaths.

He was pulling it out carefully. Once he dropped it onto the bed, he slipped his hand down my back, following the length of my spine until his thumb brushed over my stretched rosette, sliding in easily. He held it still.

Xander rose from the bed and went over to our bags, retrieved the small sack that held the various plugs.

After pulling one out, he dropped the sack onto the bed. He held it up. "This one is next, sweetheart. The biggest one. Then you'll be ready. You'll be taken by the two of us, together."

I couldn't miss their eager looks as Tyler slid his thumb in and out a few times, then pulled out. He stood and went to the basin to wash.

"We'll play with this one after breakfast," Xander commented.

XANDER

"It's the only way to lure Ralph out into the open," Emily said. She placed a tureen of soup in the middle of the table. While the cook made the meal, Emily couldn't sit idly by and let the woman serve us.

Since Tyler couldn't sit idly by and let Emily serve *us*, he brought a loaf of bread on a cutting board to the table along with a bowl of fresh butter.

"There's no way in hell I'll allow it," I countered, drying my hands on a dishtowel. The very idea of my wife using herself as bait to pull that asshole out of whatever woodwork he lived in was *not* going to happen. "I'll agree to staying here in Helena to do so, but you're not going to just wander the streets hoping he'll confront you."

We were at the kitchen table once again, this time for lunch. As Tyler had said, we'd kept Emily happy—and very busy—in our bedroom until after noon by teaching her to suck our cocks and to accept the largest plug. She was an avid pupil and we rewarded her skill and good behavior. Twice.

"Why ever not? He can't do anything if I am in public."

She was naive as to the way of desperate, corrupt people. I was glad for it, otherwise she would be like me, bitter and jaded. In the past few days though, I'd felt... better. It was amazing when I had to focus on someone else instead of myself. I had someone to live for, to cherish and protect, just as Tyler had said. That meant I would be extra vigilant with Emily, for I wanted no harm to come to her. Was this love? I had no fucking idea, but it was... good.

"She can be with me." Belinda came into the kitchen. She seemed to know what was going on without having been in the room. Having known her for several years, I'd dismissed the notion that she had special abilities, instead placing her skill at knowing everything that happened under her roof to being a mother.

Tyler and I stood, then returned to our seats when she sat and reached for the ladle.

"We will go shopping. It has been a long time since I've enjoyed that with Olivia." She looked to Emily. "It will be a treat for me."

"So I'm to have my mother and my wife at the mercy

of an extortionist?" I was glad to have Tyler agree with me.

Belinda waved away her son's gruff concern.

"Before the two of you start blustering nonsense about danger, your fathers will be home tonight and can help. If they return early enough, perhaps you can go to the saloons with them, see if you can find him."

"I thought you said you wanted us to take Emily to bed," Tyler countered.

"You have the rest of the day." His mother arched a brow at his contrary tone. "Then, later, have Xander stay here with her. Go to the saloon with your fathers. A celebration of marriage. Talk up your bride. This man, Ralph, might know that she married, but it's doubtful he knows she married both of you."

That was true. A good perk of having two husbands. One to go out and find Ralph, the other to stay and protect their woman.

"What am I supposed to say, I wore her out?" Tyler asked. "To my fathers? That seems unlikely."

I saw Emily flush.

"A late bachelor party. It's common knowledge that your fathers have been away. It's only right that you three celebrate." Belinda waved her hand through the air. "Pretend you're drunk, let your fathers watch and see if he follows. Surely, he'll want to know where you live. Make it easy for him."

The idea was sound. I liked the part best where I would stay with Emily. It was the only time I knew she'd be safe.

"Tomorrow then, for shopping," Emily added, wiping her mouth with her napkin. "I've only shopped at the mercantile. This will be... fun."

Fun was not the word I would have picked, but if Emily wasn't afraid or worried, then that was what was important. If Tyler and his fathers were able to catch a glimpse of Ralph then we'd know his intent to confront Emily again. We'd be ready this time.

16

Xander

I was buttoning my shirt when I met the men as they came in the front door. I'd heard them approach the house, their voices loud like those who'd had too much to drink. Tyler had his arm over one of his father's shoulders, laughing at something he said.

Once the door was closed behind them, the pretense slipped.

I shook both of Tyler's fathers' hands. They were both in their late fifties. While their hair was more gray than dark, they would not be men I wished to bother. They were powerful in town and had built the large ranch that Tyler and I now ran. I'd known them for years and they were the fathers I never had.

"Well?"

"First, congratulations on your marriage, son," Roger Tannenbaum said, slapping me on the shoulder. He didn't do it lightly. "It is good to see you smiling."

I couldn't help the grin, for I'd just left a sleeping and well pleasured bride. While Tyler was out with his fathers, I'd spent the time tending to Emily. While I itched to get Ralph behind bars, I'd enjoyed my evening's activities probably more than Tyler had his. "Thank you," I replied.

While they smelled of cheap whiskey, none appeared drunk. "Let's go into the office and have a drink. And not rotgut."

I followed the men. As Roger poured, the others took seats in the comfortable armchairs. Allen had raised Olivia after her parents had died, under the pretense of being a bachelor, all the while being in a plural marriage with Roger and Belinda. He had lived elsewhere with Olivia until a man set fire to their house. Then, Olivia had married Simon, Cross and Rhys and Allen chose to move in—finally—with his own family.

"I saw him," Tyler said as Roger handed me a glass with two fingers of whiskey.

My fist clenched around the glass at his words.

"From what Tyler said, this man needs to be taken care of," Roger commented, taking a sip of his whiskey.

"Hell, yes," I replied.

"We need to let the ladies go shopping," Roger admitted. I could tell he wasn't pleased with the idea either.

"You'll let him confront them?"

"Absolutely not!" Allen said, slamming his glass down on the desk. "They will shop, we will follow. Xander, you can watch the women with me and Tyler and Roger will grab the bastard before he even gets close."

I shook my head. "No way. I want the man. Emily's my responsibility."

Tyler leaned forward, placed his elbows on his knees. "Are you sure you want to tangle with the law?"

I looked at my friend closely, saw concern there. It was time I let my past go. Emily was my future and I had to ensure nothing—or no one—got in the way. "For Emily? Absolutely."

EMILY

"What do you mean, they went after Ralph?" I asked, placing the pile of boxes containing my purchases on the entry table. My voice was shrill, my heart beat frantically. I couldn't help it. The idea of Tyler and Xander confronting the man scared me. The enjoyment of shopping with Belinda disappeared and was replaced by fear. "We need to go to them. Stop them!"

Tyler's fathers, both formidable men themselves, didn't seem concerned about it in the slightest.

"No, Emily. They want you here safe," Allen said, taking my arm and guiding me into the parlor.

"They weren't supposed to go after him!" I countered, turning to face them. Belinda was tugging off her gloves and paused.

All three of them frowned. "What did you think they would do when the plan was to lure Ralph out into the open?"

I shrugged my shoulders and paced. "I thought he'd come up to me and I'd tell him that Xander and Tyler knew what happened, that it wasn't a secret any longer. He'd leave me alone."

Roger offered me a kind smile. "Do you think he'll ever leave you alone? He might threaten to tell the authorities about what you did, or perhaps Tyler and Xander's business associates."

I never considered that. My idea was all at once ridiculous.

"He won't stop, Emily. You have to know that," Allen added.

"Then I should leave them. They don't need this kind of burden. I don't want their business hurt. I don't want *them* hurt." My throat burned with tears.

"You're too upset. You're not thinking clearly," Belinda said softly.

I was brushing my hands over my skirt, fiddling with the fabric.

"You don't think your husbands can defend themselves from one man?" Allen asked.

I thought of Ralph. He was no competition physically, but that didn't mean something bad couldn't happen.

"I... I guess so, but he's... he's *mean*."

"Darling, you have to trust that your men will take care of this. That they will take care of you." Belinda placed her hands on my shoulders, looked me in the eye, then pulled me in for a hug.

I cried then, realizing in that moment how much I cared for Xander and Tyler. I hadn't wanted one husband, let alone two, now I couldn't imagine not having either. They were risking their lives for me.

Then there was Belinda and Roger and Allen. God,

they were wonderful. They were parents. Real parents. There was so much I hadn't even known I'd been missing. It took two men to show me what real love, real commitment was like. Caring. Protection. Devotion.

I saw it in the way Allen and Roger looked at Belinda, cared for her. I felt it with Xander and Tyler.

"I don't want them to be hurt," I murmured. "I don't want Xander to go back to jail."

"Xander won't be going to jail. Ralph will," Roger said. He was so sure of himself, of my husbands that it offered me some comfort.

Realizing I was a blubbering mess, I wiped my eyes and stepped back. Roger gave me a handkerchief.

"You love them," Belinda commented.

I looked to her as I wiped my cheeks, saw the pleased smile on her face. "I don't know. I'm not really sure what love is. Frank, my first husband, wasn't... nice."

Allen came over, placed a gentle hand on my shoulder. "It's love, dear. You've got those two boys in knots. I've never seen Xander so... fierce before. And Tyler, well, he's more worried about Xander keeping you for himself than anything else."

My mouth fell open. "Why would Tyler worry about that?"

"Have you seen the way Xander looks at you? He

needs you in a way Tyler doesn't. You soothe something in Xander. We can all see it." Belinda looked at her men and they nodded. "We've known him a long time. It might not be lightning, but it's... special."

"I want Tyler, too!" I admitted.

They laughed. "Of course, you do," Roger said. "Just remember, just because they're big and bossy doesn't mean they don't hurt, too. Be... gentle with them."

I thought of Xander's words, how he'd said he could never be gentle with me. While he touched me, he wasn't gentle. I craved the rasp of his callused palms. The press of his body into mine. The dark bite of his voice. And yet he was out slaying my dragons for me. He was ridding me of my one heavy burden—Ralph. It might not be gentle, but it was what I needed. What our little family needed.

I was about to respond when they came through the front door.

I stood and spun around, saw that they were in one piece and ran out of the parlor and into their arms.

I took deep breaths, savoring their scents. With them standing so close to me, it was a mix of peppermint, leather and pure male. Their hands roved up and down my back, over my hair as I wrapped my arms around them both.

They pushed me back far enough to look at me.

"You've been crying," Xander said as he glanced over my shoulder at Tyler's parents.

"We didn't make her cry. You did," Allen said.

Xander looked down at me and frowned. "We made you cry, sweetheart?"

I nodded, then smiled. "I... I love you," I admitted.

Both men stared down at me with utter shock on their faces for a moment before something shifted. Their looks changed. Xander's eyes narrowed, his jaw tightened. Tyler's looked the same, but I saw something almost reverent there as well.

Xander bent and tossed me over his shoulder and went up the stairs. His arm banded over the backs of my thighs. I wasn't going anywhere and this time—carrying me like a sack of grain—I didn't resist.

"What about Ralph?" Roger called.

"Jail. We'll share details later," Tyler said. I saw his legs as he followed us up the steps. "Emily comes first."

I didn't hear any response from below, but Xander made quick work of the stairs and we were down the hall, our bedroom door kicked shut before I could even think straight.

Instead of being placed on the bed as I'd expected, Xander slowly lowered me to my feet, my body sliding down the entire length of his. My nipples pebbled at the hard feel of him.

"Is he really in jail?" I looked between the two.

"He is," Tyler said with a resolute nod of his head.

"I didn't know you were going to go after him," I admitted.

He frowned. "What did you think we'd do?"

"I'd talk with him. Reason with him as you watched from afar."

Xander spun me back to face him, gripped my arms. He even bent at the waist so our eyes were level. "There's no reasoning with that bastard. If you think we'd let you get within ten feet of him, then you don't know the first thing about either of your husbands."

A dark intensity burned in his dark eyes. A fierceness that wasn't directed *at* me, but was *for* me.

"I am... I am just starting to see that," I replied. "Our marriage, I wanted it because I *needed* your protection."

"If you think we'll give you up now because Ralph's in jail—"

I cut off Tyler's words. "No. That's just it. I married you so you could save me, but I want to keep you because this," I waved my hand in the small space between us. "This is so much more."

"You saved us right back, sweetheart," Xander admitted.

I frowned. "How could I save you? Look at you both. You don't need saving."

The idea made me laugh.

Xander scooped me up and sat down on the bed, settled me into his lap, my head tucked beneath his chin. "You are so brave. So strong. Me?" He gave me a quick squeeze. "Not so much. I let what happened to me in the past have a hold on me, a cruel grip, that made me bitter and miserable. I was content living on the ranch away from people."

"He was downright cranky," Tyler added. He came to kneel before me. "He's not that grumpy anymore, is he, baby?"

The corner of Tyler's mouth tipped up and I smiled. "He's still bossy," I admitted.

Xander angled me back so I was staring up at him. His face, while all harsh angles and planes, wasn't... rough as it had been even a few days before. It was clear in his eyes that he wasn't haunted any longer.

"You like me bossy."

I swallowed, thinking about all of the ways he was bossy. "Yes, I do."

"As for me, sweetheart, I grew up with two fathers. They groomed me to the custom and I wanted to share a bride. I had no brother to do that with, but Xander became my brother. Not by blood, but a bond much stronger."

He looked down and I saw some of his confidence

slip. "I see the two of you together, how you respond to his touch, to his command. I'm not like that."

"I don't need two husbands like that. Xander's enough that way, trust me."

Xander lowered his head and kissed me, a quick brush of his lips over mine. It was more of a tease than anything else. He sat me back up and tucked me into him again before I could even think to ask for more.

"You balance each other. You balance *me*." Reaching up, I stroked Tyler's cheek. "I want both of you. I *need* you."

"You said something different downstairs. Do you regret the words?" Xander's body stiffened beneath mine, afraid that I would take my feelings back.

I remembered Roger's words; while they were both big and brawny and brave, I could hurt them with just a few words. The power I had was almost dangerous.

I moved from Xander's hold and turned to stand before them. I took Xander's hand, then Tyler's. "I can't really say I know what love is. Well, I never *knew*. What I feel for you both is... is amazing. Scary. Powerful. I'd say that's love."

Tyler tugged me into his arms. As he was still on his knees, he titled his chin to look up at me. "Baby, I love you, too."

"Don't forget me," Xander added, turning me into

his embrace. I cupped his jaw, the beard soft against my palm. "You're exactly what I didn't know I needed. I love you."

"It's time, baby. Time to show you what it can be like. Both of us, together."

17

Emily

My pussy clenched at his words.

"We've trained your ass," Xander added. "You take the largest sized plug so beautifully. You're ready for my cock in your ass."

"We're going to fill you right up, baby. Both of us at the same time. Do you want that?"

"Do you want to be taken by both your husbands?" Xander continued. "You'll connect us. You're what makes this family."

There was only one answer. "Yes," I replied breathlessly.

That was all I had to say before their hands were on

me, undoing the buttons of my dress, pulling the pins from my hair, stripping me bare, just as they'd stripped my emotions so they could see all of me.

When I stood before them, my nipples hard and my arousal slick on my thighs, I murmured, "I want to see you, too."

Tyler grinned, his hands going to the buttons of his shirt. "You want us naked too, baby?"

I nodded and licked my lips as I saw the broad expanse of his chest become exposed, one button at a time.

They stripped off their clothes with a ruthless haste until they stood before me deliciously naked. Xander's body was so deeply tan and sprinkled with dark hair. He was as hard as his temperament. Sinewy muscle corded his forearms, his fingers long and blunt. His cock stood thick and erect from his body, curving upward to touch his navel, a glisten of his arousal sliding down the flared crest.

Tyler was leaner, yet his muscles even more defined than Xander. His chest was free of hair, the flat nipples dark. His stomach was smooth and ridges defined it. I itched to stroke my fingers over those tense muscles. His cock, too, was long and thick, pointing straight at me, eager to be inside me.

"Are you ready for us?" Xander asked.

I licked my lips. "Yes," I whispered.

"Show your husbands," he added.

I frowned. "How?"

"Touch your pussy. Good girl. Are you wet?" Tyler spoke as I did as he bid.

I gasped at the hot feel of my flesh, eager for being touched, played with. Used.

"Show us," he added.

I held up my fingers so they could see my arousal thickly coating the tips.

Xander groaned deep in his chest. "Up on the bed."

I scooted past him and crawled into the center of the bed, laid down on my back. "Spread your legs for me, sweetheart. You know which part of you I want."

Bending my knees, I placed my feet on the soft blanket and spread my knees wide. Both men's eyes locked onto my pussy, bare and wet and swollen for them.

"You want to lick my pussy," I told him.

With one foot on the bed, Xander knelt, then lowered himself so his shoulders pushed my thighs even wider apart. "What does Tyler want?" he asked, his hot breath fanning my folds.

"My breasts." My voice was breathy and light.

"That's right, baby." Tyler came around to the side of

the bed, moved so he could cup one breast in his palm and began stroking the nipple with his thumb.

My muscles relaxed and I closed my eyes, settling in to just the feel of the men's hands and mouths on me. They touched me everywhere, my skin awakening and tingling with each pass. My nipples tightened impossibly, the painful pleasure of Tyler's fingers pinching and tugging at them, his mouth gently soothing afterward. Xander was so gentle, almost ruthless with it, barely touching the tip of his tongue to the side of my clit, around it, over it. His fingers didn't dip inside, but just lightly circled my entrance. My inner muscles clenched down, but he gave me nothing to clutch.

I was being teased, mercilessly. Instead of bringing me to a swift climax—they seemed to like to see the proof of their skill on my body—they built me up, higher and higher. My blood thickened, my breathing became erratic, my skin slicked with sweat. They were making me desperate. I knew that's what they wanted, for me to forget about everything and just feel, just react to them. Soon enough I'd have both their cocks buried deep inside me and they wanted me ready. Eager. Frantic.

Tyler moved so that he was settled on his back beside me. "Climb up on me, baby."

Xander helped lift me up and onto Tyler so I straddled him. With a hand at the base of his cock, Tyler held himself still as I shifted and moved so that he slid in easily, one long, smooth stroke. I was fully seated when my thighs rested on his.

I couldn't help the groan that slipped from my lips at how he filled me. He nudged the entrance to my womb with a small bit of pain. Using my knees, I shifted and adjusted to accommodate all of him.

Tyler's hands settled on my breasts, cupping and playing with them as I began to ride his cock. I circled and slid up and down him, using his cock for my own pleasure. The flared head stroked over sensitive places deep inside, building the burn. My head fell back, my hair tickling the length of my back.

"It's so good. Tyler, I... I'm so close."

I gasped when Xander nipped the spot where my shoulder and neck met. "Not yet, sweetheart. Remember, we control your pleasure."

Tyler removed his hands from my breasts. They felt swollen and tender and ached for his touch.

"Give me a kiss," he said. I leaned down and he wrapped his arms about my shoulders, one hand cupping the back of my head.

Tyler's tongue delved into my mouth, sliding in and out just as his cock was moving within my tight sheath.

I was surrounded by Tyler, overwhelmed by him. Joined.

A big hand stroked down the length of my spine and moved further, over my bottom and then between, brushing over my back entrance. I startled, but I heard Xander's voice soothing me as Tyler began to thrust his hips up into me, to kiss me.

You love it when we play with this virgin hole. You come for us so hard.

I settled, listening to his words, feeling his gentle touch. I felt something cool and slick coat my entrance, making his finger slide easily inside.

"That's the lubricant, sweetheart. I'll get you nice and slick, just like when we fill you with the training plugs. That's one finger. Fuck, woman, you're squeezing it so hard." Xander's voice took on that hard quality that I liked.

"Her pussy's squeezing my cock, too," Tyler breathed.

I looked down at him, saw a bead of sweat slide down his temple. His jaw was clenched and I could tell he was holding back as Xander began to prepare my bottom.

When I felt his fingers slip away, then the broad head of his cock pressing against me, my eyes widened and I felt a moment of panic.

Tyler stroked a hand over my hair. "Shh, let him in." I stared at him, focused on his face as Xander nudged against my entrance, then retreated, again and again. My breathing quickened and I worried that he wouldn't be able to get in.

I'd been fucked with the training plug in me, but never two cocks. There was a definite difference in feel, as if I was being opened so wide. I winced, then gasped when Xander pushed past the ring of muscle with what felt like a silent pop.

There was a slight burning sensation along with the stretching and I tried to wiggle away, but there was no place to go. I was well and truly impaled on their cocks. Xander's heavy breathing matched his motions, in, out, in, out, gaining more and more ground until he was in all the way.

"Oh, God," I moaned.

Xander was at my back, the hairs on his chest tickling my back. Tyler was beneath me. Both their cocks were embedded deep inside me. We were one. I was the one that connected us together, not only as a family, but in this moment, physically as well.

There was nothing coming between us. We were one.

"It's time for us to move, baby," Tyler murmured. He looked over my shoulder and gave a slight nod. He pulled his hips back, his cock sliding almost all the way out of my pussy before starting to move back in. When he did, Xander retreated, his cock sliding deep inside my ass and lighting it up. Nerves and pleasure I never knew existed came to life with his dark strokes. They worked me in tandem; one slid out while the other filled me up. Again and again they alternated fucking me until I was lost. I had no coherent thought left, only feelings. Only pleasure and deep, heady sensation that flared to life by their very skilled cocks.

I clawed at the bed as my body shifted against Tyler's, my nipples rubbing against his sweaty chest. The sensations coalesced into a tight ball starting in my pussy and ass. It built bigger and brighter, spreading throughout my entire body. My fingers tingled, my toes felt numb, my muscles went taut as my breath caught in my throat. I froze in place, trapped between my men as they fucked me, their cocks pushing me into orgasm.

This wasn't a gentle nudge as Xander could do with the flick of his tongue on my clit. This wasn't a sharp nip of Tyler's teeth on the tip of my nipple. This was them claiming my entire body. I would have screamed if it hadn't caught in my throat, the feelings coursing through my veins so powerful I could do nothing but grip the bed to anchor myself.

They didn't stop moving as I came. In fact, they

fucked me harder, driving into me, nudging my clit and forcing the climax to go on and on and on.

"She's squeezing me. I can't hold on," Tyler breathed, just before he stiffened beneath me, holding his cock deep and still inside me. I felt his hot seed pulse from him, coating my pussy, filling me to overflowing until I felt it seep out around him.

Xander didn't relent, but placed a hand on my hip, his fingers tight against the bone there as he stroked once, twice more deep in my ass. I swear I felt his cock thicken inside of me just before he groaned. In my ass, I felt hot splashes of his release.

The sounds of our ragged breathing filled the room. The musky scent of fucking filled the air. Our skin was damp and slick, my pussy was sticky with the seed that was dripping from me.

Finally, finally, Xander loosened his hold and carefully slid from me. I hissed at the last bit of stretch, then felt his seed as it seeped out. Xander's hands about my waist were what lifted me off of Tyler, pulling me off his spent cock. I was too replete to move, too overcome. Tyler climbed from the bed and returned with a warm cloth. Both my men held my legs open as Tyler cleaned me, the gentle touch of it soothing my tender flesh.

"How do you feel?" Tyler asked, looking up from my pussy.

Their Reluctant Bride

I couldn't help the silly smile that formed. "Well used," I replied. "My husbands are the most attentive sort."

Tyler grinned. "We would be happy to be this attentive again soon."

"You did beautifully, sweetheart, taking both of us." Xander pulled the sheet up and over me. "And we thought you were a reluctant bride."

"Perhaps at first," I commented, thinking back to just a few days ago. So much had happened, so much had changed in such a short time. I was no longer the hurt, scared widow. I was once again a bride. "But I am no longer a virgin. You both were my first."

Both men loomed over me, their faces—one light, the other dark—held sweet attention and love.

"Yes, we took your virgin ass, well and good," Xander said.

"And we took you together," Tyler added.

"There's just one thing left," I replied.

Both men frowned. I lifted my hands and cupped each of their jaws.

"A baby," I told them.

Both of them smiled brilliantly. "If you're not too sore, we'll get on that right now."

The idea of having a dark-haired boy or a fair-haired girl had my body softening and eager for them.

"Yes, please. Right now," I replied, nudging my legs wider, not the least bit reluctant at all.

WANT MORE?

———

Read an excerpt from Their Stolen Bride, book 7 in the Bridgewater Ménage Series!

———

EXCERPT - THEIR STOLEN BRIDE

MARY

"Up on your hands and knees, darlin'."

The man stood beside the bed, naked as the day he was born, stroking his very hard cock. Clear fluid seeped from the tip and the wicked grin on his face proved he was having a very good time. He was attractive, slim, muscled, and his jaw was darkened by a trimmed beard.

The woman smiled coyly at him and did as she was told. She wore only a blood red corset, the top few stays undone and her abundant breasts spilling out.

I stood in the next room, looking through a small hole, my hands pressed against the wall, watching. Chloe, one of The Briar Rose's many whores, stood

Excerpt - Their Stolen Bride

beside me, our shoulders bumping, as she watched from her own secret spot.

The whore, now up on her hands and knees, thrust her bottom out and wiggled it, inviting the man to look at her pussy. While neither was shy and one was a professional, they had a way about them that indicated they'd been together like this before.

I'd been eavesdropping with Chloe over the past few months and could now tell such things. Yes, I knew the more vulgar terms for a man's member, a woman's secret place and more. Cock, pussy, ass, cum. Those words were no longer crude or salacious. I'd visited the brothel, at first innocently enough to bring used clothing as charity through the Ladies Auxiliary, but met Chloe and returned out of friendship. And, admittedly, because I was curious about what went on in a brothel. What went on between a man and woman.

I gasped as the man spanked the whore on the bottom, a bright pink handprint blooming on her pale flesh.

"See, Nora likes it," Chloe whispered.

There was no doubt the whore knew of the peepholes, but the man who'd paid for a tumble with the plump Nora probably did not. They were meant as a safety measure—men were unpredictable and sometimes cruel—but I found them useful for

Excerpt - Their Stolen Bride

eavesdropping. Miss Rose, the Madame, seemed content with my *reasonably* innocent activities, just as long as I remained in hiding.

"She likes to be spanked?" I whispered back. I could see she did, with her surprised look, then hooded eyes. I liked it too, but I didn't dare say that to Chloe, or to anyone else. The idea of a man's hand striking my bare bottom made me wet between my own thighs, made my pussy clench, just like Nora.

Her pussy was pink and swollen and slick with her arousal. No doubt mine was as well, and I was just watching. I wanted a man to do that to me. Not the man with Nora, but *some* man. My man, whoever that may be. I wanted to glance coyly over my shoulder at him, see his wicked grin in return. I bit my lip to stifle a moan when he spanked her again, the loud crack of his palm against her flesh resounding through the wall.

I'd seen whores who were pretending with men, acting out their pleasure in exchange for money. But Nora didn't need to feign a thing with him. Instead of putting his cock inside her—fucking her, as Chloe called it—he knelt on the bed behind her and put his mouth... there.

"Oh lord," I whispered. Chloe covered a giggle with her fingers. I looked at my friend, all wild red hair and

Excerpt - Their Stolen Bride

pink cheeks, and I knew my eyes were wide. *That* was something new to see.

"He likes pussy," she whispered.

I put my eye back to the peephole when I heard Nora's cry of pleasure. He was licking her woman's flesh, sucking on it, nibbling, too. Oh my. His beard began to glisten with her arousal.

"That's it, darlin', come for me," the man said. "Come on my fingers and then I'll fuck you."

"Yes!" Nora cried. The man wiped his mouth with his free hand and slid his fingers in and out of her as she writhed upon them.

It was hard not to squirm as I watched the man give Nora such pleasure. He was so eager to see to her come that he delayed his own need. I wanted that. I wanted a man who put me first.

The man spanked her again. The man's cock was engorged and dripping, clearly in need of his own release. "Now, darlin'. Give it to me now."

Nora did, crying out her pleasure. The look on her face was exquisite. Wild abandon. She thought of nothing but the bliss the man wrung from her body. The man's wicked grin inferred his power over her body.

God, I wanted that. I ached for it. Needed it. But I wasn't a whore at The Briar Rose. I was a copper heiress and I shouldn't even know about fucking. I shouldn't even know the word itself. But I did. Did that make me a wanton? Probably, but my life was so plain, so strict and dull, that visiting Chloe and discovering an entirely new world was the only thing that gave me amusement. Hope.

Hope that there was a man out there who would want me like this man wanted Nora. I wanted to be wild, not stifled. I wanted to allow every one of my secret desires to be shared with someone who would see to them, not crush them beneath the boot of polite society.

I wanted more than I'd ever get with my intended husband. If my father had his way, it would be Mr. Benson and he would *never* spank my ass, or lick my pussy, or even take me from behind as the man was with Nora. Instead, I'd lie on my back in bed, it would be dark and Mr. Benson would lift my nightgown and rut into me, filling me with his seed. It would be awkward and uncomfortable, sticky and messy; I'd see no pleasure. I'd see... nothing.

When the man and Nora had found their final pleasure, both of them vocal about it, Chloe and I turned from the wall. Another whore, Betty, stuck her head into the empty room where we'd been spying. "Mary, your man is here," she whispered.

"Mr. Benson?" My heart skipped a beat at the idea

Excerpt - Their Stolen Bride

he may have seen me. Highly doubtful, but unnerving nonetheless. "He's here?"

The idea of watching my intended fuck some other woman made me nauseous.

Betty nodded, but she wasn't excited. "Yes, and he's taking a whip to Tess."

Chloe and I glanced at each other and hurried after Betty. Panic filled me at what I would witness through a different peephole, for I knew then and there that if I married Mr. Benson, the pleasure Nora had found would never belong to me.

GET A FREE BOOK!

JOIN MY MAILING LIST TO BE THE FIRST TO KNOW OF NEW RELEASES, FREE BOOKS, SPECIAL PRICES AND OTHER AUTHOR GIVEAWAYS.

http://freeromanceread.com

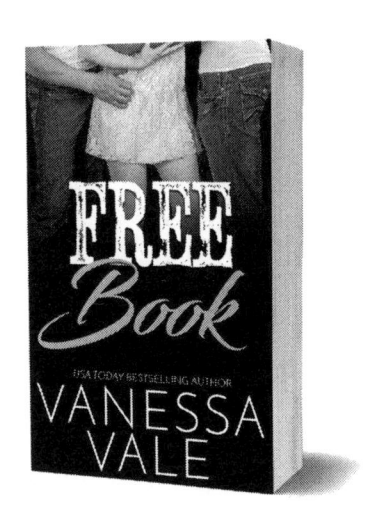

ABOUT THE AUTHOR

Vanessa Vale is the *USA Today* Bestselling author of over 40 books, sexy romance novels, including her popular Bridgewater historical romance series and hot contemporary romances featuring unapologetic bad boys who don't just fall in love, they fall hard. When she's not writing, Vanessa savors the insanity of raising two boys, is figuring out how many meals she can make with a pressure cooker, and teaches a pretty mean karate class. While she's not as skilled at social media as her kids, she loves to interact with readers.

BookBub

Instagram

www.vanessavaleauthor.com

ALSO BY VANESSA VALE

Bridgewater County Series

Ride Me Dirty

Claim Me Hard

Take Me Fast

Hold Me Close

Make Me Yours

Kiss Me Crazy

Mail Order Bride of Slate Springs Series

A Wanton Woman

A Wild Woman

A Wicked Woman

Bridgewater Ménage Series

Their Runaway Bride

Their Kidnapped Bride

Their Wayward Bride

Their Captivated Bride

Their Treasured Bride

Their Christmas Bride

Their Reluctant Bride

Their Stolen Bride

Their Brazen Bride

Their Bridgewater Brides- Books 1-3 Boxed Set

Outlaw Brides Series

Flirting With The Law

MMA Fighter Romance Series

Fight For Her

Wildflower Bride Series

Rose

Hyacinth

Dahlia

Daisy

Lily

Montana Men Series

The Lawman

The Cowboy

The Outlaw

Montana Maidens Series

Claiming Catherine

Taming Tessa

Dominating Devney

Submitting Sarah

Standalone Reads

Western Widows

Sweet Justice

Mine To Take

Relentless

Sleepless Night

Man Candy - A Coloring Book

The Alien's Mate: Cowgirls and Aliens

Manufactured by Amazon.ca
Bolton, ON